M.D. CONFIDENTIAL

(IT'S ALL VERY HUSH-HUSH...)

*To Daphne,
all the Best,
[signature]
Feb/21.*

LAWRENCE E. MATRICK, M.D.

M.D. Confidential (It's All Very Hush-Hush)
Copyright © 2020 by Lawrence Matrick, M.D.
www.lawrencematrick.com

Cover designer: Edge of Water Designs, edgeofwater.com
Interior Formatting: Edge of Water Designs, edgeofwater.com

ISBNs:
978-1-77374-057-7 (Paperback)
978-1-77374-058-4 (E-book)

Bellevue Publishing
Vancouver, BC, Canada
Printed in USA

DEDICATION

To my wife, Jean, and also to our children: Marilyn, Diana and Michael for their love, encouragement and support while writing this book and for travelling with me on this journey.

ACKNOWLEDGEMENTS

With gratitude and appreciation to my editor, Michelle Balfour.

CONTENTS

"We make a living by what we get, but we make a life by what we give."

– Winston Churchill

INTRODUCTION

This book is about the impact of mental illness; not only on the individual affected, but on their family, friends, community, and society in general. These fictional stories of various mental ills illustrate the impact on those personal lives, but also on the workplace and our educational and legal systems, causing turmoil for families and disruption for our society. Our understanding and treatment of physical illnesses has developed over time, but unfortunately research and treatment of mental illnesses has not had the same benefit.

After fifty years in practice, two years before I closed my office as a psychiatrist in downtown Vancouver, I met with the parents of a young man who had just died a week earlier of an accidental overdose of fentanyl and cocaine. For the sake of anonymity, I'll refer to him as "Jacob."

Jacob's father was depressed. Over the years he had often rescued Jacob from living on the streets in the Downtown Eastside, took him home, fed him, and cleaned him up. His son always left a few days later to join his malnourished, drug-addicted girlfriend living in a tent city at a local park.

I agreed to see the father and his second wife, the boy's stepmother, for an evaluation as to how they were coping after such a tragedy and what treatment the family may need. They left after the hour, stating that they could manage, and the father accepted a prescription for a mild anti-depressant.

As they left the stepmother turned to me and asked, "Is this all very confidential, Doctor? You know, just within these walls?" I assured her that was so, but then she whispered, "Can we keep it that way? I wouldn't want our neighbors or the rest of my family in Montréal to know about Jacob, poor dear."

Jacob's father murmured something and took his wife by the arm to lead her out. I said good-bye to them, and that the father should set another time for a follow-up. He said he'd call soon and mumbled something about putting an obituary notice in the local newspaper.

The mother looked at me again and whispered, "No. No obit notice. You know ... out of sight out of mind, and just between us now, Doctor. Let's keep it kinda quiet—you know, sort of hush-hush, please."

This book was written because mental illnesses are "kept kinda quiet:" swept under the carpet, seen as an embarrassment, and set aside. "Sort of hush-hush." However, there has been a great deal of news lately about mental illness. It is now being referred to as "psychological disorders," "stress illness," "emotional dysfunction," and other such inoffensive and innocuous nomenclature in an attempt to hide the words "mental illness."

This recent drive about mental illness has come to the fore possibly due to the recent opioid crisis and loss of life by overdose with the addition of fentanyl. The focus on mental illness must be maintained in order to dispel the stigma of this illness in our society. We must reconsider our attitude toward addictions and substance use disorders, since hundreds are dying every week throughout Canada and elsewhere. This is devastating to families and to our communities.

Statistics reveal that just over 40% of Canadians will have a mental health problem or illness, and many of these will apparently arise while the person is working. Some common illnesses that affect so many include overwhelming stress in the workplace, anxiety disorders, depression, and post-traumatic stress disorders (PTSD). Stress disorders and PTSD are now overwhelming the first responders who deal with suicide and death from the opioid crisis.

Mental health issues have also risen in prominence in our school systems. Children are now more prone to anxiety, depression, and post-traumatic stress disorders due to family disruption, a history of abuse, and, more recently, gun violence. Educational systems need more safe havens in schools with counselors who can provide psychological therapies for such students.

Included in this book are also a few sexual disorders because such disorders, specifically sexually transmitted diseases (STDs), have once again become widespread, almost pandemic, throughout all societies. The infected persons are overwhelmed with stress, anxiety, depression, and other mental health issues. Like STDs, other examples of illnesses that disappeared years ago and are again very common (due to a number of factors very well publicized) are measles, chicken pox, whooping cough, mumps, and HIV. STDs are now difficult to treat, since antibiotics are less therapeutic than they were, and they are again rampant due to carelessness and ignorance.

Surprisingly, health statistics reveal that STD transmission among the elderly is now a common problem. Between 2007 and

2011, chlamydia infections among Americans sixty-five and over increased by over 30%, and syphilis by just over 50%. This year cases of congenital syphilis have been confirmed in this province alone. Overall, rates of infectious syphilis have increased in males and reproductive-age females. Now it is recommended by the Centre for Disease Control that all pregnant women are screened for syphilis during the first trimester of pregnancy or at the first prenatal visit, as well as at delivery. A chapter on congenital syphilis is included.

STDs have long-lasting mental and psychological complications like severe anxiety, stress, panic, and depression, and for that reason have been included here.

The last chapter is on gender dysphoria, commonly referred to as a sexual identity change, which is now frequently discussed in the popular press. This was included since it also causes such intense anxiety and mental anguish for those affected, including the parents, families, friends, and even for society as a whole as we attempt to understand the reasons, implications, and consequences.

THE HISTORY OF MENTAL ILLNESS

The history of mental illness reveals that the mentally ill have always been shunned in all societies throughout history. They have always been with us, and will be for a long time to come.

Such disorders were well-documented by the early Greeks, Romans, and Egyptians thousands of years ago. Those who hallucinated, heard voices, and expressed fear of others (that is, they were delusional), were considered to be very special and have the ability to see into the future. They were revered as extraordinary due to their psychotic manifestations.

Several hundreds of years ago, it was decided that the public had to be protected from such deranged individuals, but also that they required protection from the abusive public. Thus they were housed in mental institutions.

The first written knowledge of such intuitions came from the Arab Islamic states, as explained by travelers to those areas. Cairo had such a hospital in the 9th century for the care of the insane and employed compassion, support, and music therapy as treatment.

In medieval Europe, the insane were housed in some monasteries, small villages, and in city towers called "fools' towers." The hospital in Paris, Hotel-Dieu, had a few cells in the basement solely for lunatics. Also, the Teutonic Knights had hospitals with small attached "madhouses."

In 1285, a treatise by Sheppard, "Development of Mental Health Law and Practice," described a case of a "frantic and mad" individual due to "the instigation of the devil." Thus, such illness was then associated with Satan.

Spain had many institutions, and in London, England, The Priory of Saint Mary of Bethlehem was built in 1247—later known as the famous Bedlam.

Much later, throughout England and Europe, the parish authorities assisted families both financially and with nursing care for their mentally disabled. Such a parish might further help by housing a mentally ill family member in a private madhouse or board them out with other caring families. Some charitable institutions, supported by religious groups, were available, such as Bedlam.

In the early 18th century, many cities throughout England had private institutions. Unfortunately, there are recordings of some institutions selling or renting out their patients in the form of slavery. Such individuals served as serfs in various workhouses, mills, and mines. In the early 19th century, the College of Physicians in England put a stop to that practice.

Privately-run asylums developed in the 1600s, and in 1632 the Bethlem Royal Hospital in London recorded that in the lower levels there was "a parlor, a kitchen, larders, and several rooms where distracted people were held." Those who were violent were chained, but all others could roam about and even had access to the public areas close by.

When King George III had a remission of his mental disorder in 1789, such disorders were finally seen to be treatable and curative.

Moral and compassionate treatments prevailed with the French physician, Philippe Pinel, in 1792 at the Bicêtre Hospital near Paris. Pinel and others freed patients of chains and dark dungeons were abandoned. It was agreed that such illness was the result of social and psychological stress, hereditary tendencies, or the result of physiological damage. Attendants and other nursing personnel were taught to be compassionate, supportive, and humane. Patients were encouraged to work in the hospitals and on discharge were assisted within the public workplace.

In England particularly, cottage-like homes developed to house those requiring less supervision. Such cottages held 50-70 patients, and it produced a familial environment, where patients were encouraged to perform chores to allow a sense of contribution. They were rewarded with Christmas, Easter, or other holiday incentives.

I and my wife, a nurse, had the opportunity to work in such humane and modern cottage hospitals at the Runwell Hospital in Wickford, Essex and St. Ebba's Hospital in Epsom, Surrey in the early 1960s. I was surprised that at Easter, Christmas, and other festive occasions the women received a small glass of sherry and the men a small tankard of beer at mealtime. They were light-years ahead of the huge, red brick, four-story monstrosities that held four to five thousand patients in Canada and throughout the United States.

In the USA, the first psychiatric institution opened in 1773 in Virginia: the Eastern State Hospital. Later, in the early 19th century, many such hospitals opened throughout the States.

In Canada, every province had immense, three-to four-story ornate hospitals. Each building was fronted by magnificent

Corinthian columns, and some contained grand staircases. However, a few levels had bars on the windows, and many had padded cells. Each was a community within itself, and in the 1960s they became more civilized with beauty parlors, cafeterias, movie houses, game rooms, private showers on each ward, and overnight sleeping rooms for families from afar who came to visit their relatives.

I myself worked at the Weyburn Mental Hospital in Saskatchewan in the summer of 1951, the Brandon Mental Hospital in Manitoba in 1956, and then at Essondale, later called Riverview, in British Columbia in 1958 and again in 1961 and 1964. I was impressed with the caring, supportive, and considerate attitude of all nursing, medical, and personnel ancillary care.

In the 70s and early 80s, there was an international movement to decentralize such large institutions and move patients into their communities to be with their families. Thus, group homes were established. Patients were encouraged to be treated at home with therapists visiting close by. Outpatient units were attached to every medical facility in the area.

However, many patients were unable to adapt since they had been uneducated, unemployed and had no training whatsoever. There has been an outcry by the public, since many such patients have been seen to be on the streets, addicted to drugs and alcohol, and sleeping in store fronts, parks, or alleys. The prisons now house many mentally ill individuals. Housing for the poor, the destitute, the indigent, and the mentally ill is obviously wholly inadequate.

It is important to realize that institutionalized patients before the 1970s were generally very well cared for. Prior to their hospitalization, many mentally ill were unemployed, uneducated, shunned, isolated, rejected, abused, exploited, or addicted to drugs and alcohol, and upon their discharge, many unfortunately returned to their old habits.

With hospitalization, they received good medical attention, proper hygiene, adequate nutrition, and companionship. Many worked in the kitchens, laundry, libraries, and farms, or as gardeners, aides to mechanics, assistants to the nurses and medical staff, cleaners, barbers, and hair stylists. They formed close, lasting bonds with the staff and with each other, and often had supportive family visitation, occupational therapies, and regular religious spiritual assistance.

Such hospitals often had festive nights with food, music, and even dances, especially during special occasions. Once weekly, a hospital had a movie night held in large auditoriums, and occasionally such patients were entertained by outside groups of performers.

With the "progressive" drive to close such hospitals throughout the world in the 70s, all such patients returned to receive "treatment in the community," and were moved into halfway houses or to be with their families. As to treatment, they saw a counselor, nurse, or a psychiatrist once per month for fifteen minutes to readjust their medication. They remained poorly prepared for life outside of the institution: unemployed, shunned and isolated in the community, and left on social welfare.

Many became "the homeless" on the streets: addicted to drugs and alcohol, behaving in anti-social activities, prostitution, and often subsequently suffering imprisonment. Change requires a large amount of funding for rehabilitation, re-education, close supervision by counselors and therapists, treatment facilities, and better housing. Such change requires greater advocacy, raising the profile of mental illness and the need for open public discussion by individuals and community groups.

"Nobody escapes being wounded. We are all wounded people, whether physically, emotionally, mentally, or spiritually. The main question is not, 'How can we hide our wounds?' so we don't have to be embarrassed, but 'How can we put our woundedness in the service of others?' When our wounds cease to be a source of shame, and become a source of healing, we have become wounded healers."

– Henri Jozef Machiel Nouwen

ADDICTED ALLISON

"Hey, Simon. That bitch daughter of yours, Allison, has taken our new clock radio, my good pillowcases, and my brand-new suitcase out of her room," Adele, Allison's step-mother, shouted down from the second-floor landing.

"Damn, I never even heard her get up and leave, Adele. We shouldn't have taken those sleeping pills last night," Simon shouted back as he made coffee for the three of them that morning.

Adele came into the kitchen frothing at the mouth. "No point making her coffee, Simon. She'll sell my good cases and my radio on the street to get more coke. She'll be drinking that rot-gut on Sherbourne Street. Or shooting up on Queen, Dundas, George, or in Regent Park with that no-good Nazi bum of hers. You know, that coke head, Vongrubber."

"It's Gunther. Her boyfriend, Gunther."

Simon poured a coffee for Adele and tried to calm her down. "December is a cold month, Adele. At least she has Gunther to help her sometimes. I'm afraid she'll end up with pneumonia again, like when she almost died last year in hospital. I'll go look for her tomorrow, since it's the weekend."

Adele sat down, sipping her coffee but pounding her fist on the table. "You shouldn't have given her that money, dummy. She'll just shoot up with that German fucker of hers and peddle her ass on the weekends. You're just enabling her by giving her money. He takes it off her to buy more smack to shove up his arms or snort more snow up his nose."

Simon knew that was the way it was. "Well, she's my daughter, Adele. I have to try and find her, and at least get her and Gunther into an addiction clinic. You know: some good therapy."

Adele stomped out of the kitchen and yelled out from the hallway, "Yeah, well, she should get a life, Simon. Pull herself together, get a proper job, and stop wasting our and the government's money every time the police pick her up or the ambulance takes her to the hospital. You know, to clean her up." She slammed the door to the kitchen but had a parting shot. "She doesn't have a pot to piss in, Simon … my God, and she's piss-poor. You keep giving her money. Simon, the enabler!"

Simon followed Adele out of the room, trying to placate her. "You keep saying she's piss-poor, Adele. Where does that saying you use so often come from?"

Adele smiled for the first time. She was on stage again, with her university degrees plastered all over the kitchen walls and her part-time acting career. "Now listen up, Simon. In ye olde England, some had a metal pot under their bed. There were no toilets or bathrooms, so they pissed into those pots all day and all night. When the pot was full, they took it to the leather tannery factories in the city."

Simon clapped his hands as he recalled. "Aha. Yes, England was awash with beaver and other hides from America, and the uric

2

acid in urine was needed to tan the hides into leather."

"That's right. They sold their urine for a few pennies or florins. However, if they were very poor and couldn't even afford to buy a pot, then they didn't have "a pot to piss in" and were really "piss-poor.""

Simon thanked Adele for the lecture, but she still berated him as he left. Simon left his third wife at home and finished his day working as an accountant that Friday, but he had to travel to Ottawa that week to do some contract work for the government.

On the next weekend he got into his car, turned on the wipers to clear the sleet coming down, and headed for Regent Park in Toronto. "This is where I usually find her. Pray to God she's there," he said to the radio announcer talking about a snowstorm hitting the east.

After two hours of circling the park he gave up. "There, I see her friend, Gunther," he suddenly shouted out as he rounded a corner onto Dundas.

Gunther was negotiating with two men in black windbreaker jackets and hoods pulled over their heads. Simon recognized Adele's clock radio held by one of the scruffy characters.

He stopped his car on the busy street. "Hey, Gunther, where's Allison?" Have you seen her? I'm looking for her."

Gunther came over to the open window. He was unshaven, wearing a dirty toque pulled down over his sad, grubby face, and his breath stank. "Yeah, yeah. She's upstairs. In number six. She's okay, I think. She needs a fifty. I'll give it to her," he said, showing Simon the dollar bills and hiding the syringe and needle with his other hand behind his back. He smelled of booze.

Simon looked up at the seedy rooming house with a body sleeping on the open doorstep. Cars were honking for him to move on.

"I'll be right back, Gunther. Tell her I'll help her." He started his car and drove around the block to find a car park. That took an hour. He paid the attendant and walked back to look for Allison at the "The Swank Rooming House" on Dundas.

He stepped over the body at the door that was ajar and pulled back the thin sheet, praying that it wasn't his daughter lying there. It wasn't, but the body had a cardboard sign next to it. "A few pennies for Penny, please." He threw some coins into the empty jam jar.

He waited for some response from Penny. When he got none, he called 911 and reported the body. "No, she's alive," he said and left.

He walked into the "The Swank." A hooker approached him and asked him if he'd like a good time. He brushed her aside, held his nose from the stink of cheap perfume, and walked up two flights of stairs to find number six.

The door was slightly open. Simon walked in, not sure what he would find.

There she was. Allison was sitting on a chair, just barely conscious, swathed in the two pillowcases and a ragged, filthy, moth- eaten blanket. The room was small, cold, and stank of marijuana and stale cigarette smoke. The one small window was covered in sheets of old newspaper, and the only table held an old, grimy, dog-eared bible. There was an old electric heater in the corner sitting idle. He walked over, plugged it in, and turned it on full blast. It spluttered and died.

He came back to his daughter. "Allison. Are you all right? What are you doing?"

She sat in a soiled, white plastic chair and was trying to work on her laptop, which was propped up on a yellow card table that was badly stained with cigarette burns. Simon was appalled to see her so tired-looking and indifferent.

"Hey, pops. You found us. Doing design work for the movie company in town, working on the blue screen for a backdrop. Good job, pops. Good job. Pay's good," she answered not looking up.

Some time ago, Simon had told Adele that he was proud of the fact that Allison had graduated from her graphic design course last year at the local college. It was after he had last rescued her from hooking on the streets. As usual, Adele had chided him for bringing her home and cleaning her up again. "You spent all that money for her design courses and what did it get you? Nothing but more trouble."

At that time, Allison had told Adele and her father that Gunther was a graphic artist in Frankfurt, and together they hoped to find work. Adele had just laughed out loud. Simon knew that Allison was also a very talented artist but that talent was never used.

Simon looked about the room at "The Swank." The walls were covered in sheets of sceneries of old Toronto painted by Gunther. Gunther was snoring on the floor in the corner on a frayed mattress. He had vomited and stale urine filled his pant leg.

Simon put his hand on his daughter's shoulder. She winced. "Come home, dear. It's almost Christmas. It will be warm for you," her father said kindly. He looked over at Gunther and cautiously added, "Maybe bring him when he's off drugs, and both of you can see a counselor. Come home, you know, for some turkey."

Allison brushed her father aside. "Naw, pops. He's got some good work now and cleaning up. I'm off all that junk, and Gunther found us a nice, clean place to live. Somewhere over there," she said and pointed somewhere to her left.

Simon shivered in the cold, damp room as he looked at Gunther again. He didn't think Gunther would clean up, nor that she would get off all that junk, stop hooking, or survive until Christmas.

He pulled his coat around his body to keep warm, tired, often in pain, and dreading retirement. Adele was threatening to leave him if he brought "that no-good daughter of yours home one more time." He couldn't keep looking for and rescuing her. He was feeling his age, and his arthritic hip needed surgery. He ambled down the stairs and found his car.

Allison's father worried about her throughout December. He had nightmares of her lying on the snow-swept streets of Toronto, and he couldn't concentrate on his work. In the first three weeks of that month he avoided driving around Regent Park, Queens, Dundas, and Sherbourne. Occasionally, he called his friend on the police force and the emergency ward at the hospital to see if she had been admitted.

Finally, two days before Christmas, he succumbed to his night terrors and despair and drove to the dilapidated rooming house. As he walked up to unit number six, the hooker sitting on the floor in the corner was snoring softly. She looked much older.

This time, the door to unit six was locked. He knocked on the door. An elderly, grizzled man with a cigarette dangling from his lips opened the door and peered out.

After reassuring the man that he wasn't a cop, Simon asked what had happened to the man and woman who lived there.

"Ah, yeah. Nice lady. Gave me her card table and mattress. Moved," he answered, still fearful. Then he recalled, "Moved, she said to me, she said. To the Majestic Hotel. On the good side of Dundas, she said. The good side." He pointed far behind him, somewhere over that way.

Simon walked out into the dismal street, found his car with a recent key scratch on the passenger's side, and slowly drove to the "good side" of Dundas.

A traffic cop pointed to the Majestic down the street. He found a parking spot close by and looked up at the seven-story hotel. Not so majestic, but clean and better than "The Swank." It even had a reception desk in the foyer.

Simon asked the elderly desk clerk if his daughter or Gunther were registered. The kindly old lady nodded, checked her books, and told Simon that Gunther Schmidt and his wife were in 704. "Take the elevator to seven and turn left," she said.

He did that, knocked on the door, and was met by Gunther Schmidt. "Gunther? How are you? Is Allison here? The lady at the desk spoke of your wife," he asked, trying desperately to stay calm and not punch him in the face.

"Ha. Come on in. How'd you find us? Naw. No wife. The desk didn't accept singles. Too many addicts and hookers around. Didn't want those types in here," he said, pulling Simon in.

Simon looked around. The one-bedroom unit was clean and tidy. Gunther's drawings, diplomas, and designs were neatly arranged on the walls, methodically organized. A wonderful aroma from the small kitchen of something cooking flooded the room.

Gunther went into the kitchen to baste a small turkey. "Keep basting, Gunny," Allison shouted from the bathroom. She peered out to see her father.

"We've both got good work as graphic designers in blue screens for the TV and movies, Simon. We can pay you back now," Gunther shouted as he pushed the bird back into the oven.

He walked out and pulled up another chair for Simon at the table. Gunther was clean-shaven, dressed in designer jeans, a clean, button-down jacket over a blue shirt, and expensive shoes. Simon looked at the open bible on the table. It was open to Luke 15 and the story of the prodigal son. The son who was lost for years but returned to the open, loving arms of his father.

Gunther came to Simon and whispered, "We're both in therapy at the addiction center, thanks to you putting Allison up to it some months ago. Both clean and sober. Good jobs, too," he said proudly as he moved the bible away.

Simon patted Gunther on the back, but he almost swooned to see Allison come out of the bathroom. She wore a beautiful dress, make-up, and high heels, and her hair was streaked a soft blonde.

Allison came to her father and gave him a warm hug. "Hi, pops. I knew you'd find us. Come have some turkey. Merry Christmas, pops."

Gunther looked at Simon. "Your wife will be angry that you found us. She'll complain that this will now cost you more money."

"No, I'll cope with that. It's like that passage in the bible. Lost but found again."

Allison laughed as she put cutlery on the table. "Yes, Dad. But not the prodigal son. It's the daughter," she said and pointed to her sketches on the wall behind him.

He turned to find several beautiful pencil sketches of street people: eating, walking the alleys, sleeping in doorways, and shooting up. He recognized Penny with her cardboard sign.

Allison beamed, adding, "I didn't want all of them to be invisible to our city manager and Premier. The government keeps all this poverty too hush-hush."

Gunther took Simon's arm and led him to the table, now nicely set with a tablecloth and cutlery.

Smiling, Allison took a parcel off the table and handed her dad a present wrapped in brown paper with a red ribbon.

He opened it to find a framed sketch that she had designed and signed at the bottom. Simon put on his glasses. It was of a man sitting at the fireplace in a big easy chair. A little girl sat on his knee, and he was reading her a story. She was looking up at him lovingly, holding onto his hand.

Tears welled up in his eyes as he recognized that the sketch was of him and the little girl was his daughter. As they did years ago, at bedtime.

SUBSTANCE USE DISORDERS

In the above fiction story of a young woman with addictions, Allison, the word "addiction" is commonly used to describe a brain disorder (as some medical specialists refer to it), or as a mental/psychiatric condition. Her addiction and her addicted friends had a profound impact on her family, but also on society as a whole in its legal and socio-economic aspects.

To be more precise, the American (and Canadian) Psychiatric Association categorize "addiction" as a Substance Use Disorder. This disorder is a medical condition where the use of substances leads to a clinical impairment or distress. Such distress produces mental, physical, or behavioral effects, and causes loss of control, stress to the mind and body, tolerance, and severe withdrawal complications.

Such intake of substances that are addictive, rewarding, and strengthening cause dependence. Dependence is a state related to withdrawal on termination, and this, in turn, produces catastrophic symptoms to the mind and body.

Substance use and abuse is commonly referred to as drug abuse, drug addiction, and chemical dependence.

There is a multiplicity of mental/psychiatric disorders associated with substance use. Such specific mental disorders are multiple, but commonly include all of the psychotic disorders like delusional formation (false beliefs) and hallucinations (hearing voices). Anxieties, depressions, sleep and sexual dysfunctions, delirium, and cognitive malfunction (memory, confusion, disorientation), can also be included.

Drug classes that produce substance use disorders, including dependence, are many, but common ones are alcohol, stimulants (like meth), cannabis, hallucinogens (like LSD), opioids, hypnotics, and anxiolytics (some tranquillizers).

Vaping is now a serious addiction, causing pulmonary problems and death, apparently due to the lipids and various oils used to produce taste and smell, which then interfere with breathing.

Marijuana has been legalized in Canada and in other countries. It now has the potential to produce serious complications, both psychologically and cognitively. That is, for anxiety and depression and for memory, orientation, and the thinking process—especially in adolescents and younger adults.

The medical associations in Canada have advised women to avoid cannabis while pregnant or while breast feeding. There is added concern that cannabis may reduce the fertility rate for both men and women and affect their offspring.

The Diagnostic and Statistical Manual of Mental Disorders (DSM-V) describes dependence as when a person persists in use of addictive drugs despite their problems. Compulsive use may cause tolerance, and withdrawal symptoms occur when use is reduced or stopped.

Tolerance means the diminishing effect of a drug resulting in the repeated use at a given dose or increasing the dosage. Dependence is an adaptive state that is associated with a withdrawal syndrome experienced upon cessation of repeated exposure to a drug. An addictive drug is a drug that is rewarding, strengthening, reinforcing, and supportive for the individual.

The causes of substance use are multiple, but it is reported that children born to such parents have a higher degree of risk. Some suggest that it could be genetic or behavioral. Young people in their teens, depending on multiple factors, may continue using drugs well into adulthood.

Other contributing factors are being male, having other mental health problems, lack of family or community support, and lack of supervision.

Physical dependence affects one's physical and mental health, and is characterized by symptoms of physical withdrawal, like tremors or sweating, and psychological dependence with emotional-motivational fears and anxiety symptoms.

Diagnosis usually requires a complete examination by a professional. At least several ongoing clinical symptoms must be present. This could include using a drug more than originally required, (i.e. tolerance), cravings, and intense urges to use. Also required is the inability to reduce or stop using, working hard to find the drugs, stopping one's usual healthy activities like work and education, and the avoidance of close, meaningful relationships.

Management and therapy may include partial hospitalization with medical detoxification by professionals. This is in order to prevent delirium tremens and other severe physical withdrawal symptoms. Many may seek or agree to therapy, but there is a high risk of relapse. Recovery may depend on mental health issues that can be readily treated by professionals.

However, ignorance of the circumstances that the individual is in, plus a lack of personal desire for change, may make treatment very challenging. Ongoing social problems, personally rigid characteristics, and major psychiatric illness requiring hospitalization can all be problematic for therapy.

In the past few years, the statistics reveal that a small percentage of early teens have an addiction disorder due to the availability of meth, cocaine, and now, fentanyl. There is also a higher incidence of those between the ages of eighteen and twenty-five. Some authorities report that in the USA there were over seventy thousand deaths from drug overdose, especially in younger adults, in the past year. The death rate from synthetic opioids like fentanyl has increased sharply, as has death from heroin and cocaine. It can be difficult to describe the cause of mortality due to the use of multiple drugs. However, many authorities still claim that tobacco use is still a major cause of disability and death.

In some Canadian provinces, the death rate from addictions has almost doubled in the past several years, and there has been a major increase in motor vehicle accidents due to driving impairment from drug abuse.

It has been reported that fifteen hundred have died from drug overdose in British Columbia last year alone and there has been an increase of death in homeless people due to drugs.

Articles written by addiction therapists report that the life expectancy in Canada and the US has decreased due to deaths from alcohol and drug use and the resultant high suicide rates. This is especially a factor in those living in the lower economic strata.

Indigenous people also have disproportionately poorer mental health outcomes. They are over-represented in social, health, and in the legal services.

Mental health issues from addictions include severe anxiety and depression, manic disorders, panic, and severe cognitive memory symptoms. Those who "crash" from overuse are exhausted, withdrawn, despondent, and may have physical symptoms like high blood pressure, tremors, and shakes. They require immediate hospitalization and treatment.

Alcohol is the most common, and most frequently abused, substance and the most socially acceptable world-wide. Unfortunately, moderate to heavy intake produces a higher sense of confidence, good feelings, light-headedness, and sociability. But soon after the typical hangover begins with headaches, fatigue, gastrointestinal problems, and indifference to the person's social surroundings or apathy to their personal relationships.

Fetal Alcohol Spectrum Disorder has become a serious illness, and some statistics reveal that a million Canadians alone now have this disorder. It is the result of women drinking alcohol while pregnant, which produces a brain disorder for the child still in the womb. Such children have mild speech problems, memory defects, and severe cognitive delays. Their futures can be devastating with unemployment, homelessness, addiction, and abuse.

As dependence and addiction progresses, a person loses their self-control, with impending violent behavior to others or physical harm to themselves. Ongoing heavy drinking leads to severe destructive behavior, agitation, general malaise, and extreme physical symptoms like heart failure, stomach bleeding, kidney dysfunction, and brain/memory distortions.

Withdrawal from alcohol can induce severe physical and

mental problems, and typically the DTs (delirium tremens) require immediate medical assistance. In such traumatic stages, one's life can be threatened due to psychosis with hallucinations and delusions (hearing voices that are threatening and false beliefs that can be destructive to oneself or to others).

Alcoholic dementia or chronic severe cognitive disorder is not uncommon. Seizures and total collapse can be lethal. Immediate treatment with hospitalization is essential.

Other very common addictive substances are nicotine, caffeine, cocaine, stimulants and amphetamines (speed, meth), hallucinogens (LSD, mushrooms), marijuana, inhalants, opioids, fentanyl, and some sedatives that can produce serious consequences.

Cannabis users have a higher risk of sedation, lowered blood pressure, dizziness, and memory distortion. Each one of these complications can alter close relationships, social interaction, educational endeavors, and the operation of a vehicle or a bicycle. Cannabis intake can precipitate severe anxiety, depression, or psychotic states, especially in those who are more vulnerable because of existing personality issues or a past history of mental health problems. The young are most vulnerable to cognitive/memory dysfunction.

Addiction treatment therapists report that more addicts now die from drug overdose than those involved in car crashes. Naloxone and other medications save lives if diagnosed early, except with fentanyl overdose, where severe breathing problems and brain damage occur very suddenly.

The diagnosis of substance abuse can be difficult, since such addicts can be solitary, reclusive, and protected by their compatriots, fellow addicts, or their pushers, as we found Allison to be in the above fictionalized story in such circumstances. Their lifestyles can prevent prompt evaluation due to their anti-social behavior, criminal activity, or prostitution.

Diagnosis is made when the individual is using more of the substance than originally planned, is unable to cut down, has a high craving, is unable to meet social and employment obligations, causes harm to others, needs increased amounts, and eventually has withdrawal symptoms.

Diagnosis may depend on whether the symptoms are significantly distressing or include obvious impairment with a physical or psychological disorder. When consumption is overwhelming, the individual's health deteriorates with constant pain, confusion, nausea, and often fatal dehydration. The final diagnosis will require a complete history, a thorough physical evaluation by a professional, laboratory testing, and admission to an outpatient clinic or hospital.

Other more contemporary addictions are becoming problematic. Examples include obsessive use of the internet, personal communications with smartphones (e.g. texting, selfies) and other self-centered, narcissistic activities. Many young people go to bed with their phones nearby, breathlessly waiting for a communication from a friend.

The glaring light of a phone or laptop at bedtime is very stimulating to the brain, and not conducive to a restful sleep. The ensuing daytime fatigue and the use of cell phones while driving is now a major cause of accidents.

Addictions to food and sugary drinks producing obesity are now another serious concern, as is the addiction to online gambling. Such behavior is a major financial loss for many families. Binge-watching TV or streaming services contributes to poor sleep habits, insomnia, increased fatigue, and unhealthy eating habits.

The combination of sedentary activities with the above food

addictions has led to weight gain, visual and cardiovascular illnesses, and diabetes.

Treatment must be prolonged with ongoing individual and group therapy under supervision by professionals in a recognized facility to assess mental and physical health disorders. Lengthy follow-up is essential, with involvement of close relationships (marital or otherwise) and with family members.

Often remission is short-lived and severe relapse can cause death. Death happens because the addict goes back to using the same dosage they used prior to remission. That dosage is often mixed with fentanyl and can be overwhelming to the mind and body, with lethal results.

Treatment facilities have been overwhelmed by substance use disorders. There is a greater need for governments to authorize adequate funding to educational institutions for professional therapists. There needs to be more services, especially for marginalized people.

Fortunately, there has been more research, understanding, and awareness of the potential to recognize and treat substance use disorders. Those who enter treatment and have interpersonal, familial, and community support with extensive follow-up have a more favorable prognosis.

There has been a movement in the popular press by addiction specialists and others to decriminalize all illicit substance use. Thus the addict would not be the criminal, and the money spent on prisons would be used to fund pharmacological and psychosocial intervention, housing, and other harm-reduction strategies.

STRESSED MIGUEL

Miguel broke out in a sweat. His mother had scolded him throughout his youth for scratching at his face, twitching uncontrollably, and walking in his sleep. "You've forever been an anxious child, unable to suckle properly at birth, biting your fingers, scared to go to sleep, and scratching at that nervous rash on your face."

This morning his heart was in his throat. He was on his way to the airport to greet his ailing mother, flying in from Cuba. He hopped up and down from one foot to another at the bus stop.

Finally he saw the bus with an airport sign pulling up to his stop at Portage and Main Street in Winnipeg.

"I haven't seen my mother since I was a young teenager, and I'm so nervous," he said to the kindly lady bundled up in a heavy parka standing next to him. They patiently waited as the first snowfall of mid-October enveloped the group. They huddled together as the north wind blew down Main Street.

She muttered something in Hungarian and nodded, but slowly moved away as he moved from side to side, mumbling. He wasn't going to tell her anything else, as he was afraid that she would see the red rash on his left cheek.

He never told people that his father had secreted him on that fishing boat years after Castro took over all the tobacco plantations. He had been a young rebel, helping his father, but was slated for prison for moving the Cuban cigar seed out of the country. After nearing Florida, the Cuban gun boat had rammed his father's trawler and sunk it. The ten others on board didn't survive, but he was a good swimmer in high school and had made it to shore. He never saw his father again, and that trauma triggered his frightening nightmares forever after.

He looked at the immigrant lady and had some empathy for her, since he was grateful to Canada for accepting him. He was proud of his new citizenship.

The bus slid to a stop on the icy road and everyone hustled aboard. "Will this bus take me directly to the airport?" he asked the driver as he hit his head with his fist to shake the traumatic memory away. His memory returned to the present as a young tough pushed past him.

He put his coins in the box as the driver started up again. "Yes, mister. Hang on to the straps. The bus is full, and the streets are slippery with all this snow falling."

Miguel wanted to use his cell to call his wife in Elmwood and tell her he was on his way. He let go of the overhead strap as he took out his cellphone. Other passengers jostled past him to get to the back.

He heard the bus driver yell something. Miguel saw the garbage truck swerve into Portage Avenue at the crossing and slide right through the stop sign.

The bus driver slammed on his brakes and swerved left to avoid the truck. Miguel saw the accident about to happen. He shouted, stopped breathing for a minute, dropped his cell, and fell forward. He slammed his head into the metal coin box near the door.

It was then that he had the flash of memory again. It was his father's boat, torn apart by the gun ship and sinking on the coast of Florida.

He could hear the bus driver somewhere far off in the distance. "Are you okay, mate? Injured? I'll call an ambulance." Two strong young men picked him up. One put his handkerchief to the cut on his forehead to stop the bleeding.

"No, no. No ambulance. I'm okay. I need to get ashore with the others. My father can't wait; he'll be arrested," Miguel answered, dazed. He was confused, with the past traumatic memories from his youth flooding his mind.

"What'ya say, buddy?"

Miguel shook his head, dabbed the blood away from his right eye, and pushed himself up. He thanked the driver and the two men. He assured them that he was unhurt as he searched for and finally found his cellphone under a seat.

Passengers behind him urged the driver on, shouting that they had to get to the airport on time. A young lady got up and offered him her seat.

The bus did get him to the airport on time, and Miguel met his mother at the arrival gate. After many hugs and kisses and a selfie photo, they took the bus, laden with suitcases and many tired travelers. They sat together holding hands, and she commented on his sweaty palms, as usual.

The weather had turned cold, and a snow blizzard choked the roads. "Maybe, my son, maybe your mama should'a stay in Havana," his mother said as she covered her head in the woolen shawl that

Miguel gave her.

On the way home, Miguel's fingers were painful from gripping the seat handle so tightly and holding his mamma's old suit-case on his knees.

"Miguel! What is it? You are so nervous. Is it me, Miguel?" his elderly mother asked as she looked at his pale, ashen face.

Miguel didn't answer; he was too preoccupied with the traumatic memories of the fishing boat sinking, the loss of his father, and the drowning of his friends years ago. Then that truck hurtling toward the bus on the way to the airport and hitting his head on the coin box. And now his mamma's presence next to him, reminding him of his fears in Cuba, his youth, and his renewed anxiety.

That night, once his mother was settled and his family had listened to her stories, he stayed awake until the wee hours of the morning. He was plagued with recurrent memories of his childhood, flashbacks of the near-death accidents and vivid nightmares in Technicolor of sharks nibbling away at his feet off the coast of Florida.

That next morning his wife, Esmeralda, shook him awake. "Wake up, Miguel. Wake up. The bed sheets are wringing wet. You were shouting out to someone, kicking as though you were swimming, and trembling all night. What is the matter, Miguel?"

Miguel sat up, cleaning the sweat from his face with the bed sheet. "Esmeralda, you must help me. I am suffering from those disturbing memories and dreams. Someone at the clinic I went to called it PTSD. I was dreaming about the accident on the bus and the past events that have repeated over and over after I got my memory back."

Esmeralda sat next to him and hugged him. He explained that he felt anxious all the time and his head ached. He would break out in a rash all over his body. His muscles felt tense, and his heart raced. He was often short of breath, and he developed stomach problems. His interest in sex had just totally disappeared and he told her he felt guilty about that.

She reassured him and held him close. "I'll take you back to our doctor later today, Miguel. He'll refer you back to that clinic. Your dear friend told me yesterday that you need a good psychologist again for all that craziness you've been telling him. Your other friend, Carlos, said that you must be a nutcase, and he laughed at you."

She did take him to see the family doctor that afternoon. He confided in Dr. Ricardo, an elderly father-figure also from Cuba, that he was losing weight and complained of diarrhea.

The doctor prescribed a tranquillizer, but when he returned home Miguel continued to feel exhausted all the time. He became very depressed. His nightmares were horrific—he kept having flashbacks of riding a bus that was flipping over or on fire or careening off a cliff. His concentration was affected, his memory was poor, and he couldn't focus or multitask. He felt a constant sense of fear of reliving the near-death experiences.

As time went on, he couldn't continue as a construction worker. He was $60,000 in debt, his ten credit cards were maxed out, his bank loan payments were due, and his wife could no longer support the family with her part-time job at the restaurant. His mother was helping out by babysitting for the neighbors, but his line of credit was coming to an end. The pills prescribed by the doctor didn't help.

Financially, he was now dependent on his friends, having cashed in his RRSPs and an old insurance policy. His family doctor saw him again and prescribed sleeping pills and samples of another anti-depressant.

He told Miguel that the psychologist he had seen only once

last month had reported back that he was suffering from post-traumatic stress. She had suggested that Miguel seek long-term treatment with medication from a psychiatrist.

"No, no, Doctor. I'm not crazy. Just a bit tense. A bit nervous." Dr. Ricardo reassured Miguel and listened to his memories of escaping in his father's fishing boat. "And then that knock on your head in the bus. You'll see a neurologist first, to make sure you didn't have a brain injury, son. Then that psychiatrist will get you on the right meds for your PTSD."

Miguel had an MRI by the neurologist and was assured that he didn't have a traumatic brain injury. The psychiatrist's correct medication gave him calmness, a better sleep, and his appetite increased. His wife was happy to have a renewed relationship.

Finally, the referral to a psychologist for cognitive therapy added to his recovery. The boys at work were glad to have Miguel back in the New Year doing home renovations.

Carlos apologized to Miguel for his rude remarks towards his illness. He was happy to have his friend smiling again and joking about the good times they had in Havana as teenagers.

POST-TRAUMATIC STRESS DISORDER

PTSD, as this mental disorder is commonly called, can happen for anyone who is in an accident or experiences an event that is frightening and a cause of concern for that person's safety. It was originally called "battle fatigue" or "shell shock" following the great wars. Any event that produces a sense of fear, hopelessness, or helplessness with a possible threat to one's health or life can trigger overwhelming anxiety and PTSD.

PTSD is now very common among first responders like ambulance personnel, the police, medical health workers, and friends and families who witness death and destruction. It has a devastating effect on the work force economically and on society in general.

One of the criteria for diagnosis is the exposure to actual or threatened death or serious injury, sexual or otherwise. Directly experiencing such an event, being a witness to a family member or close friend, or repeated exposure can precipitate such a disorder.

Following such trauma, the person experiences distressing memories, disturbing dreams, flashbacks, severe anxiety, and physical complaints. It is common to avoid by whatever means available any distressing memories or external associations and activities that can cause startle responses.

It is also common with PTSD to detach oneself from people for fear of further trauma. The need for alcohol or drugs to sedate and calm oneself down is overwhelming.

Those who witness the event or assist those who are involved in the traumatic circumstances can develop the disorder also. It is not unusual to feel stress, fear, and overt clinical anxiety with increased heart rate, nausea, or sweating if involved in a frightening situation. This fear response is your body's way of telling you to protect yourself or get out of that situation. It is a natural protective mechanism, but if it continues and you are unable to extricate yourself from the threat, then the symptoms become more permanent and fixed in duration.

Most people subjected to such physical or psychological stress usually recover in a short period of time, but if there is a history of fear and anxiety already in one's life, then the condition becomes one of severe PTSD.

Everyone feels fear when threatened, but the symptoms of PTSD are severe and crippling. They can be triggered by some inconsequential event, a dream, a statement, a smell or noise, certain words, a movie, or a vision of something traumatic and similar to what they already experienced. Miguel's reliving of his earlier trauma in Cuba when he saw the truck about to strike the bus that he was riding is an example.

Generally, there are a few different categories of physical and psychological complaints. Flashbacks are common, as are frightening intrusive memories, overwhelming anxiety, and heart, breathing, stomach, or urinary symptoms.

Others may simply avoid any situation where they perceive a threat, like driving in a car, taking an airplane, being in enclosed places or with people who are aggressive.

Some may be overly vigilant, easily startled, angry, or inflict self-harm in order to get out of the disorder. Finally, some are depressed, have memory and concentration complaints, or isolate themselves. Often, they are overwhelmed with guilt because they were the ones who survived.

Children can also suffer from this disorder, and this may not be evident to parents because the youngster hides and avoids talking about it. Thus the parent and others are unaware. Children can become frightened of being separated from their parents (separation anxiety) or have sleep problems, nightmares, sleepwalking, or complain of vague aches and pains after any traumatic event.

Some individuals are at more risk for developing PTSD than others. The extent of the frightening situation is a factor, but if the individual is already an anxious person or prone to fear, phobias, depression, or severe social isolation, then their risk is greater.

The more extreme the threat, the greater the potential for PTSD. Intent to harm like potential rape, torture, and personal assault can be of great threat to that person. If the event is unexpected, uncontrollable, and inescapable then PTSD is more certain to follow.

Individuals, especially younger children, are also more predisposed to PTSD if there is a family history of stress and anxiety. Sexual abuse, drug addictions, a past history of stress, and trauma—especially in the home—makes children more vulnerable in the future. Psychological disorders in the person or in the family structure will also predispose that person to a greater risk.

More recently, PTSD became an international disorder following military combat between nations or immigration events, mostly for those citizens involved in the conflicts. Veterans returning from combat areas were especially vulnerable. However, any type of traumatic event can precipitate PTSD such as accidents, childhood neglect and abuse, natural disasters, personal tragedies, and violence.

Other emotionally stressful events leaving a person exposed in any form (physical or psychological), and causing them to feel hopeless and helpless will trigger the response. The sudden death of a loved one, bullying, harassment, or any type of humiliating experience can seriously affect a person and make them vulnerable in the future.

The trauma of being raped or sexually assaulted, for males or females, can have an everlasting effect. Such an event can trigger fear, shame, personal isolation, nightmares, recurrent flashbacks, and memories. Often such stress may abate with time, but will again resurface, such as when legal action is taken following the event. This is due to the renewed discussion and resurgence of required memories in a court of law.

Recovery from PTSD is a very individual journey, and many can cope and recover with time, depending on their own personal strengths and familial or social supports. Such a journey will require time, and reaching out to family and friends who are willing to listen and be supportive can be therapeutic.

One can deal with such stress by helping others personally or in group therapy. This can be empowering, as it allows for the building of personal strength, and a means to deal with the sense of helplessness. Volunteer work with others who are disabled can be very helpful.

There are other many positive behaviors for coping with PTSD. Learning about PTSD, joining a PTSD group, practicing yoga, meditation and other relaxation techniques, outdoor activities, exercising, avoiding alcohol and drugs, eating a healthy diet, and socializing with positive people are all very therapeutic. Some have explained that boxing, shouting, or weight training is most helpful to release the anger and pent-up aggression.

Treatment with a professional therapist in conjunction with these personal activities can produce a full recovery. This is not a sign of weakness, and such a therapist can offer more explicit and longer-lasting therapeutic results. Prompt therapy is essential for ongoing symptoms. It allows one to strengthen family supports, deal with their anger, prevent violent and self-destructive behaviors, and build personal ego strengths.

Such treatment may involve cognitive-behavioral therapy, family therapy, and or medications. It may require some time to find a therapist who deals with PTSD; talk to your doctor, or call a mental health facility. If a veteran, then call a veteran's support line. Talk to your own doctor to assess the possibility of medication, or see a psychiatrist who can prescribe the appropriate medication to help you with the nightmares, flashbacks, sleep disorder, or other disturbing physical or psychological anxieties.

Hope for permanent recovery is possible with the above self-involved therapeutic modalities and professional treatment. Family supports and community support groups are essential. It can be kept very personal and confidential if the injured person so requires, but openly dealing with the PTSD and exposing oneself to family and friends can be very strengthening and rewarding.

JOSIE THE JUMPER

At 9 AM the bridge was finally free of the morning rush, but it was a cold day in November, with dark, heavy clouds and rain threatening in the mountains. On such a day, Reg knew that his jogging friends would be at the gym instead of running across the bridge to Stanley Park in such bad weather.

"This kinda weather is okay for me, and good to be alone," he said to a seagull soaring above him on a strong wind as he jogged along. He pulled down hard on the woolen toque on his head, zipped up his jacket, and slowly picked up the pace.

Near the halfway point, he spied a woman at the top, uppermost span of the bridge. She was looking over the rail at the tide rushing out and waving to a cruise ship sailing into the busy harbor. *Presumably another jogger watching the freighters make their way out to sea. The Holland American cruise ship is coming in,* he thought to himself.

As he neared the top level, he gasped to see her leave the sidewalk and crawl onto the railing. Reg quickened his pace, but he was too late.

As he approached, he saw that she was a middle-aged, scrawny woman, wearing dirty slacks, a t-shirt, and only one filthy runner. He slowed down, fearing that he would scare her. He watched as she scratched at her face, drawing blood, and then licked at her fingers.

Jogging faster he saw her throw her right leg over the rail, but she was too weak to hoist herself farther. Now that he was near her, he looked about for help, but the sidewalk was empty in both directions.

With great effort, she perched herself on the rail and teetered on the edge. Several cars had slowed down, and some honked their horns and swore at her.

One oaf shouted out, "Let her jump. Saves the government money." He sped off, still complaining that she was holding up the traffic.

"It's okay, buddy. I called 911," one young Asian woman called from her open window as she stopped her Lexus SUV on the bridge.

Reg waved to the woman in the car but that only got the jumper to edge herself off the rail more precariously. A slight drizzle started to cascade down on the scene, causing Reg to be more anxious as the railing became wet and slippery.

Reg moved cautiously to her side. He feared she would panic if he touched her or grabbed her arm, and then she'd be gone for good. Cars had slowed down both ways, honking and hooting. Some people had stopped behind the young lady's Lexus, and traffic in the other direction slowed to see what was happening.

The young Lexus lady had jumped out of her car and was yelling, "Hey, fella. Grab her for Christ's sake. Grab her before she jumps."

Reg felt the panic in his chest as it tightened up. His heart was in his throat. He waved the Lexus lady away and came close to the jumper. "Hold on, miss. Hold on. Wait. Don't do it," he shouted, breathless. He was aware that she was in a daze. She seemed confused: wide-eyed and staring at the swirling waters below.

He was at her side now, and ever-so-gently took her arm as she sat there teetering on the rail. She was oblivious to drivers shouting, complaining about being held up and telling her to jump. She stank of filthy, unwashed dirt, grime, and alcohol.

She tried to pull away from him, causing her to slip even farther forward. Reg grasped at her emaciated body with both arms and pulled her back onto the walkway.

It was then that another passing motorist stopped. The older man leaped out of his car, ran across the roadway—stopping one car on his way across—and jumped over the concrete barrier protecting the sidewalk to help Reg and the Lexus lady to sit her down on the walkway.

"You'll be all right, missus. I called the police, and an ambulance is on its way for you," the older man said anxiously.

Reg gave a sigh of relief as he heard the wail of sirens in the distance coming out of North Vancouver. A tow-truck made its way down the center lane and waited for the police cars and ambulance to arrive. The tow-truck man had opened the center lane, but the two outside lanes were still blocked off.

The rain had turned to a wet snow. The Lexus lady was shivering in her light blue jacket, which covered a white nurse's uniform.

The response from the jumper was immediate when she heard the word "police." She crossed herself several times, prayed to the Virgin Mary, and then bellowed out loud, "No police. No, no, no, they will lock me up like before. I'll kill myself if they lock me up again. I can't stand a lock up … shit, I panic if I'm inside. Can't be inside. Let me go!"

As the nurse helped Reg sit her up, she took off her jacket

and wrapped it around the jumper woman. A light mist off the water and the snow slowly enveloped the trio. The nurse pointed to the vacant space where her right breast used to be, indicating an amputation.

Reg saw that and gave a sad, worried look to the nurse. Still holding onto her, since they feared the woman would try to run away and jump, the nurse asked, "Why would you jump? I'm a nurse going to work. Are you depressed? What's your name?"

Reg held on to the jumper, fearing she would bolt. He felt comforted to have a nurse close by. *She'll know what to do,* he thought.

The jumper turned to look at her savior, the kindly young lady, but didn't know which question to answer first. She became very pensive. Still bewildered, she slowly replied, "My name? It's Josephine, nurse. Josie, they all call me in the park. Josie," she repeated sadly.

Reg gradually backed off from holding Josie, happy that a nurse was taking over. He could see that Josie hadn't washed for some time: as her hands were filthy, as was her face. Her nails were bitten to the quick, and her long brown hair was knotted and in a mess. Her tattooed arms were infected from needle marks.

She only had one shabby runner on her left foot; the other foot was bare. "My other runner fell off into the waters below," Josie said to Reg. Her black slacks were soiled, as was her ragged t-shirt under the nurse's jacket.

He presumed she had been sleeping in the park at the end of the bridge, like so many other drug addicts do. He'd read that they became too suspicious and paranoid, panic-stricken if enclosed in a room, and thus they felt much safer outdoors.

"You are depressed, Josie. But don't worry. If the police do come, they won't take you away. I'll make sure of that. The ambulance will take you to the local hospital. I work there. My name is Annabelle," the nurse said, kneeling close to Josie.

Reg and Annabelle got up as they heard the wail of sirens slowly ebbing. The older man backed off and waved to the three police cars. They were quickly on the scene. Two of them had stopped the traffic both ways to clear the area, but some got through down the center lane.

The other police car helped to escort the ambulance close to the four on the walkway. The deafening noise of sirens was shut down.

Drivers slowly inched their way across the bridge down the center lane, and some who were close by behind the police cars opened their windows to see what was going on. Many shouted and complained about being late for work, annoyed with the bright, red glow of lights flashing on and off.

The nurse bent down, gave Josie a hug, and brushed the tangle of hair away from her sad, forlorn face. "Just stay close to Josie," the nurse said to Reg, and then added, "I'll talk to the paramedics."

As the snow came down heavy and wet, the older man took off his hat and covered Josie's head. He left to warm up in his car as the nurse identified herself to the paramedics. As they both listened intently, she explained that Josie was in a severe state of depression and was suicidal.

They slowly approached Josie, not wanting to frighten her, and ever-so-gently escorted her into the back of the ambulance.

One of the paramedics took the nurse's jacket from Josie and gave it back to the nurse. "I'm Federico. Bryan and I … we know Josie. She's addicted to opioids and fentanyl, poor lady, and more depressed after her mastectomy. She's been in the hospital a few times, but they just discharge her back to her pusher, who she sleeps with in the parks. They both get hopped up on speed, Dexedrine and fentanyl. The speed junk seeps out onto her skin and her face.

It's Itchy, and she scratches and bleeds."

Annabelle nodded … a familiar story for her. "I've heard that one before, Federico. I may have seen her in the ER. Can't remember. So many of them, but I'll be sure to take care of her when she's admitted."

Federico explained that he knew her history from the ER physicians after so many admissions. "Yeah. Tragic. Her pusher overdosed on fentanyl and died last week. Reminds her of her father's death from drink. Her uncle sexually abused her in her teens," Federico said and then added, "Her mother abandoned her when she was only fifteen. She was depressed then, and now must be depressed over her losses. She drinks too much. Plus the junk she's on," he said sadly.

The nurse nodded knowingly again.

Bryan wrapped a warm blanket around Josie as Federico waved the police cars off. They drove away, lights flashing in the steady snowfall, now mixed with rain.

The impatient honkers, at least in the direction of the park, were glad to get to work. The older kindly man waved and drove off. Reg moved on, slowly picking up his pace, glad to leave the tragic scene.

At the bridge, two police cars had moved off and traffic resumed, much to the relief of everyone. The one tow truck operator who saw the traffic back up waited behind impatiently. He waited for the nurse to get into her car safely but shouted out to her, "I hope you guys cure those nutcases who keep trying to jump. They slow the traffic down for hard-working people who need to get into town." He pointed to the cars slowly inching their way across the bridge.

He opened the other lanes for traffic and slowly drove back toward the city. He waved to Reg as he jogged by.

Josie was taken to the ER at the local hospital, where she was quickly seen by the resident psychiatric physician. After the lengthy consultation and a quick physical she was diagnosed as suffering with a major depressive disorder, alcoholism, drug addiction, diabetes, and pneumonia. In addition, she needed further evaluation as to her cancer.

She had some insight into those disorders and readily agreed to be admitted for therapy at the hospital's psych ward.

"It will be much warmer here than in the makeshift tent where you lived in at the park. You can stay here for a few weeks for treatment, with meds by the psychiatrist, and I'll call in our psychologist for cognitive therapy for you," the psych nurse said as she helped Josie to her bed.

DEPRESSION

E veryone may feel blue or sad periodically, but depression is an ongoing, persistent feeling of despair, worthlessness, and the lack of pleasure in all activities and relationships. It is a complicated mind and body illness that prevents a person's functioning in all endeavors.

A person like Josie in the above fiction story suffering from a depressive disorder has a pessimistic outlook, suffers from a sleep disorder, has a prolonged period of inactivity, a lack of energy, an appetite disorder with weight loss, and a sense of worthlessness and hopelessness.

Unfortunately her mental illness had an impact on bridge traffic, but such a depressive illness has a major influence on all aspects of our society. In the fictionalized story she was mocked, scorned, and ridiculed by passersby on the bridge.

Depression can be precipitated by prolonged stress, multiple losses, or ongoing medical or physical disabilities. Early childhood trauma, family crises, and disruption with social loss, educational, or employment complications during the teen years, sometimes with ill health or drugs and alcohol addictions can be precipitating factors in adult life for the onset of depression. Those were the precipitants in Josie's earlier life.

Early analysts concluded that it was a defense mechanism—that is, an attempt by the body to slow the person down from further harm and to alert the mind and body to be aware and hopefully deal with the impending crisis or losses. It is not a sign of weakness, but a sign of pain so that the person can stop and deal with the causes.

Depression can be an episode and may clear with time, but if ongoing it requires some form of intervention and therapy.

Generally there are three types of depression. A Major Depressive Disorder is as it sounds … it is major. It is a prolonged mental disorder that overwhelms the whole body and mind with a persistent sad mood. It also produces low self-esteem with a loss of interest, low energy, and often a sense of bodily pain that is difficult to explain. If it becomes intense, the person may hallucinate or be delusional with paranoid ideas—that is, hear voices or feel suspicious with false beliefs.

Physically, a person with such a Major Disorder feels a lack of interest in personal relationships, avoids educational pursuits, social interaction, and the workplace. Sleep is disturbed, appetite disappears with ongoing stomach problems, weight is lost, sexual interest wanes, and general health suffers.

Such losses with severe isolation and a sense of inadequacy can lead to thoughts of suicide as a way out of the despair. Most people who commit suicide have been suffering from severe depression.

Depression often coexists with various medical conditions like aging and early dementia, pulmonary problems, diabetes, stroke, and other neurological issues or heart disorders. Children often do not demonstrate overt clinical depression, but instead act out in their despair with aggression, avoidance of school and friendships, severe dependency, early use of drugs, or other anti-social behaviors.

Long-standing chronic anxiety, panic attacks, and phobic disorders often go hand-in-hand with ongoing severe depression. Such anxiety disorders will complicate the treatment and recovery.

Childhood attention-deficit disorders can also make the diagnosis more difficult to treat. Depression usually coexists with addiction and personality disorders, especially during the dark days of winter in a depression referred to as Seasonal Affective Disorder.

Ongoing chronic pain disorders often lead to a depressive disorder, especially in women.

A second type of a very common depressive disorder is Dysthymia. It was mostly called this in the past, but is now referred to as a Persistent Depressive Disorder. Dysthymia simply means a bad state of the mind.

Essentially, it has the same symptoms as the major type of depression, but it is of a lower-grade and yet persistent. It is less disabling but can be longer lasting. Often, it is more difficult to diagnose, since the individual can function reasonably well, or just marginally, but also may have fewer physical complaints.

Thus such a person could go on for many years with the malady without proper evaluation and treatment. It may just become the person's ability to hide their problems and sense of despair, and is instead seen as part of their overall personality.

This persistent depression can become a more serious major depression if there are other major losses, and it can then have all the associated symptoms of the major type.

This persistent type can complicate cardiovascular and heart conditions and seriously affect other medical conditions like arthritis, weight gain, and diabetes, causing such conditions to continue to be undiagnosed and untreated for many years because of the person's disinterest and apathy.

The predominant complaints are a sleep disorder or sleeping too much, with a lack of energy and concentration, poor self-esteem, and a sense of hopelessness. There is an avoidance of taking any risk that may cause further failure, stress, trauma, or embarrassment. Also, there is very little sense of pleasure in social or personal endeavors.

The cause of this persistent disorder is basically unknown. Genetics is a strong factor, and a family history of a similar ailment can often be the case. An overwhelming medical condition or severe, prolonged anxiety or stress and the lack of family or social supports leading to social isolation can be a strong factor in causation. Any recurrent, fluctuating mood episodes, drug and alcohol addictions, and disabling medical conditions can precipitate such a disorder.

A third common depressive disorder is Premenstrual Dysphoric Disorder. This can be a severe and disabling syndrome for menstruating women. It occurs during the luteal phase of the menstrual cycle—that is, just after ovulation. It may end once menstruation begins, but it could last for several days thereafter. Symptoms can be both emotional and physical, but mood symptoms are predominant, specifically sadness and despair. It is a more intense form of PMS, and is cyclical and more disabling.

The cause of this type of depression is considered to be hormonal, but the cause is basically unknown. It is surmised that some women are more affected by the hormones progesterone and estrogen. A family history can be significant, but recent investigations have suggested that girls and young women who use hormonal birth control pills are more prone to future depressive disorders.

Major symptoms of depression are present just before menstruation begins and start to abate once menstruation stops. Such common complaints are irritability, anger, depressed mood, anxiety, reduced interest, poor concentration, lethargy, appetite changes, stomach cramps, bloating, breast pains, and sleep disorder.

It is important for the woman to see a family physician or specialist for a complete physical and psychological evaluation. This purpose is to determine the hormonal biochemical status with blood work, and to understand the emotional history to rule out other physical causes or rule out the longer-lasting depressive disorders described earlier.

Some other common depressive disorders are the result of a bi-polar, or commonly called manic-depressive, disorder, as well as the condition from years past called melancholia. There are some depressions that are caused by substance abuse like opioids, cocaine, or the overuse of sedatives or hypnotics. Depression can be the result of certain medical conditions like strokes, Parkinson's disorder, chronic brain injuries, multiple sclerosis, Cushing's syndrome (an adrenal condition), and hypothyroidism (a low thyroid condition).

Some individuals are affected by a seasonal pattern disorder, also called Seasonal Affective Disorder (SAD), a depression occurring regularly in the fall and wintertime during dark days. The recent use of special bright lights and lamps has been very effective, but Seasonal Affective Disorder may clear in the spring or summer months.

A less common depressive disorder called Postpartum Depression occurs for some women during pregnancy, right after delivery, or sometimes soon after. Many symptoms are those of the Major Depression as outlined earlier. This disorder may remit—that is clear up—spontaneously soon after delivery, but may require further evaluation and treatment. Assessment by a physician is mandatory if there are unusual thoughts or behaviors. Such thoughts may be those of extreme suspicion, false beliefs or delusions, hallucinations, the hearing of voices, or thoughts of suicide. Such a disorder can be dangerous for the woman or her child.

Men can also suffer from a depressive disorder following the birth of their child. Postnatal depression is not uncommon for men, but men tend not to complain about their despair and reveal it in other forms, such as fatigue, loss of appetite, weight gain, poor sleep, anxiety, physical stress symptoms, or alcoholism. They will avoid work and interpersonal relationships or resort to drugs, both prescribed and illicit.

It is important for the family to be aware and seek an evaluation, but also for the partner to make the physician aware of the situation with the new birth and the man's symptoms as stated.

The causation of any of the above depressive disorders may be attributed to earlier experiences of family or social disruptions, physical, sexual, or psychological abuse, or other prolonged stress or traumatic environments. Experiences of failure, social isolation, disappointments, the loss of health, and ongoing rejection can often be a precursor to future depression. Highly introverted personalities and those lacking skills, education, and close relationships may be more prone to depression. Some women may have a higher incidence of this disorder due to hormonal influences.

However, men may also suffer from psychic pain and despair, but may manifest depression differently. Men may have different ways of coping and may express loss through fatigue, irritability, overt anger and aggression, over-work, physical activities, drugs, and alcohol.

Women more frequently attempt suicide than men do, but men have a higher incidence of actually committing suicide successfully. This may be due to the fact that men more rarely seek help, assessment, or treatment.

Older people may be more prone to depression due to multiple losses but also due to vascular heart and stroke effects. With the loss of memory and resulting dementia, such depression is often missed or misdiagnosed.

Recent research is moving toward pharmacogenetics. That is genetically evaluating a person to understand if certain anti-depressants work better for some and not for others. Unfortunately, the use of modern anti-depressants may not be effective for some and thus a physician or psychiatrist will try different medications until one becomes therapeutic.

Anti-depressants take time to work, and therefore some patients will ask for electro-convulsive therapy. Such treatment, ECT, has an anesthetist available to calm the patient with intravenous sedation and an anti-convulsive medication to reduce muscular spasms. The use of the unipolar electric charge is more effective with fewer memory distortions and faster relief.

Readers may question the reasoning behind passing an electric discharge across the frontal lobes, thus producing a convulsion. Such a convulsion, by whatever means (fevers, leptazol, insulin, or electrical discharge) has been found to be helpful, and indeed, curative, for many mental disorders. Now it can be fast, effective, and sought after by those who are aware of its curative effects so that they can get back to work more quickly.

Over the course of many centuries, it was observed that epilepsy and mental illness never coincided in the same person. This is not factual, but if a mentally ill person had an epileptic seizure and a convulsion, then they went into remission—that is, they were temporarily better or even permanently cured of their depression or other disorder.

Years ago, it was also found that those who were deranged and had a fever from some infection with the resulting convulsion were similarly much better or cured. Fevers prior to antibiotics were common and were the result of pneumonia or various other infections, including syphilis, which was rampant in the past (and now making a startling recovery).

Over a hundred years ago, some physicians treated general paresis of the insane (GPI), caused by the syphilitic spirochete bacteria and causing insanity, with injections of malaria. The malaria illness produced a very high fever, which then produced a convulsion. It was the convulsion, the seizure, that cured the insanity.

Later it was discovered that a chemical, metrazol and leptazol, when injected intravenously also caused a seizure and was thus curative for severe depressions, schizophrenia, and other chronic mental illnesses. Insulin, when injected, severely dropped the blood sugar, which then produced a convulsion. Pumping sugary water into the stomach quickly revived the patient after the convulsion. Insulin coma therapy was very popular for many years in the treatment for various mental illnesses, especially depressive disorders.

Electric eels were used by the early Egyptians to hopefully cure a variety of neurological and mental illnesses. Centuries later, magnets and magnetism deployed on the brain were similarly used, but ineffective. When electricity came into use throughout the world, many physicians employed the current to shock musculature and the nervous system to cure such neurological deformities with questionable results.

In Italy, in the mid-1930s, two Italians, Ugo Cerletti and

Lucio Bini, worked in Genoa, Milan and then later in Rome to experiment with electric currents in the treatment of various neurological illnesses, but again with very little effect.

The manager of an abattoir invited them to help shock pigs and other animals into a coma so they could be more humanely slaughtered with the use of their electric current. They brought an ice tong, connected electric wires to the tongs, and passed a current across the pig's frontal lobes. The pig had a major convulsion but woke up, squealed, and ran off. The experiment was a miserable failure.

Despondent, the two Italians went home, but several days later the light bulb flashed, and they had a brilliant idea that lasted many decades and changed the course of mental illness treatment. They realized that they had produced a convulsion in the pigs. They asked the director of a local insane asylum if they could try their convulsive therapy on some of his patients. He agreed, having nothing to lose, and sent them to the attic where the most depraved and psychotic men were housed.

The two 'therapists' asked two burly assistants to hold down six men as they attached their electrified ice tongs to each patient's frontal lobes. They pushed the button to pass an electric pulse across the frontal lobes, and each patient had an uncontrolled major convulsion. This was repeated several times over the course of a few weeks.

At the end of two to three weeks, they came back and asked to see the patients again. They were nowhere to be found.

They were discharged, the director explained. Their families took them home. They were well and healthy, and were needed to work in the vineyards.

Cerletti and Bini were nominated for the Nobel Prize in neurology, but at that time it was awarded elsewhere. ECT treatment was interrupted by the war, but was used extensively throughout the world after 1945 and still is. It has been well-recorded that the famous writer, Ernest Hemingway, the pianist and movie actor, Oscar Levant, and TV host Dick Cavet were treated with ECT.

However, now an anesthetist is present to give the patient an intravenous sedative and a quick-acting anti-convulsive such that the only way the convulsion is detected is by a flutter of the eyelids or a twitch of the fingers. Also, the current is now unipolar to reduce any memory defect that used to be a complication. It is often requested by those who want to return to work promptly and not wait for the slower, anti-depressive medications to take effect. Time is money.

Psychotherapy with a qualified psychologist, together with the above-mentioned therapies, can have a very positive outcome for depressive disorders. Other effective modalities are exercise, participating in social or religious activities, group therapy, and having someone to confide in to reduce one's isolation. Let your family and friends help you. Talk about your feelings and your depression.

Do not keep such a depressive disorder to yourself; it should not be kept secretive. Also, let others who may feel the same way benefit from your experience. Allow yourself to be a support, a mentor, to them and a good friend.

Remember that good friends can be a strong pillar for you. Sometimes they hold you steady, or they may lean on you. Often, it's just comforting to know that they stand beside you.

ANGELO HAS THE CLAP

"Wake up, Angelo. You are hot to touch; burning up, my friend. You go see the ship doctor this morning, for sure. You heard?" Angelo's friend, Cristofer, shouted as he put on his white cotton uniform of the kitchen staff. He was in the bathroom and ready to go to work that early morning. He would follow his other two bunkmates to work in the cruise ship's kitchen and laundry rooms while it docked in San Francisco.

He turned and gave his good buddy a large bottle of water as he walked into the cramped room. "Drink this. It'll cool you off," he offered.

Cristofer then finished shaving, combed his hair, and squirted aftershave lotion all over his face. "That beauty: Serenity was her name, you said? That number nine was her number, a tag that she wore on her skimpy dress: legs apart and no undies. It was in the room with the large glass window with the other girls: how old was she? That district in Bangkok was pretty seedy, Angelo wasn't it?" He put on his white kitchen jacket and admired himself in the mirror for the last time before going to work.

Angelo's mouth was so parched from the fever that he couldn't reply. He was still angry at Cristofer for taking him to the Patpong district of Bangkok when his cruise ship, *The Orient Crescent*, docked there for three days several months ago. Once all the passengers were transferred to the buses waiting to escort them to see the elephants up the river, the crew had several hours on land to rest up.

"It's my balls that hurt, Cristofer, and I have a terrible headache from fever. Serenity? Told me she was twenty-one," Angelo said, his eyes blinking rapidly as he drank the whole bottle of water in one gulp. He slowly maneuvered himself out of the upper bunk, protecting his delicate and very swollen testicles with his left hand, and held on to the short ladder with his right hand as he slipped down it.

Cristofer looked at his watch. "Got to go, my friend. It's just about six. Twenty-one? Bullshit. Didn't look more than my seventeen-year-old sister, Letticia, still living in Manila with my mamma."

Angelo shrugged his shoulders and waddled off to the toilet. He tried hard to urinate in the bathroom now that his friend was leaving, but complained bitterly of burning as the urine flowed out. He was more frightened at the white, creamy puss oozing from the end of his penis as he squeezed it after urinating.

"Pass me my sandals, Cristofer, before you go and as soon as I finish here. I can't bend over with the pain down there in my crotch."

Cristofer did so and regretfully admitted, "Maybe that wasn't such a clever idea, buddy, to pay for Serenity when we were last docked there in Bangkok. That day we should have just seen the royal palace and the Wat Arun with the monks selling jewelry. Not those girly-girly shows or massage parlors, Angelo. Shoulda walked out, and Bob's your uncle," Cristofer said.

He wagged his finger at his buddy as he turned to go. "You go see the medic here at the ship's clinic about your pain, but tell him about you blinking all the time, also. I'll cover for you in the kitchen, and Bob's your uncle. You'll be hunky-dory once again."

"Listen Cristofer, hold up a sec. What's with this 'Bob's your uncle' thing you always use? Who the dickens is Bob?"

Cristofer stopped at the door. "Bob? Just a saying that everything will work out okay. You see, a certain Mr. Balfour, in around 1887 in England, was sent by his uncle Lord Robert Salisbury, the English prime minister—called Bob by his friends—to be the chief secretary of Ireland. Balfour, the nephew, didn't do a good job of it at all."

"So what; big deal. Lots of those around," Angelo said, smirking.

"So, the critics and all the Irish said to their friends, and then to his face, 'Listen Mr. Balfour, you only got this plush job because Bob's your uncle.' But eventually it meant that everything will work out for the best."

"Ha, Good one. So if I see the doc, then 'Bob's your uncle' and I'll be okay?"

But Cristofer had already left and Angelo, alone in the sparse four-bed bunk room, slowly slipped into his very loose gym shorts, sandals, and a t-shirt. He made his way down the long, narrow hallway of the cruise ship to the elevator and up to the fourth level where the medical clinic was.

As he entered the medical clinic, he was pleased that the ship's doctor was present, and that the waiting room was empty that early in the morning. The young, attractive receptionist opened a file on him and asked him personal details about his medical history. Then she introduced him to the aide. The nurse's aide, a pretty, middle-aged Japanese woman, Aiko Fujiyama as he read her name tag, ushered him into the examining room.

"Doctor Carrera will be right with you, young man," the aide said as she left in a hurry.

After several minutes the doctor came in, limping. He was dependent on a cane and wearing a dark brown, felt fedora pulled down close to his bushy eyebrows. He read Angelo's chart and looked at him. He raised his fedora slightly, smiled, set his cane on the desk, and then announced, "Drop your pants and underwear."

Angelo did that. Without being asked, he explained that his testicles were painful, he had a fever, painful urination, and a discharge from his penis.

The doctor was an older man, balding and with a trim beard. He had recently retired from practice in the city. Cristofer had seen him previously for his bronchitis and told Angelo that he was working part-time as a ship physician.

"Let me put on the latex gloves so I can examine your genitals, Mr. Angelo," the doctor said after reading his chart again. "You have an infection. Possibly venereal. You visited Bangkok the last time you were docked there? That's what the nurse wrote in your chart," he said as he gently maneuvered Angelo closer to his desk lamp.

Angelo only nodded, embarrassed at his pants being down as the pretty, Japanese nurse's aide walked in and watched the doctor examine Angelo.

The doctor removed his hat and shone his overhead lamp on Angelo's private parts. He whistled and said, "Clap: some call it the 'Drip.' We call it gonorrhea. Caused by the bacterium, *Neisseria gonorrhoeae*, my boy. We see lots of clap after the ships dock there, in those places. The nurse will give you a salving lotion."

Fujiyama scoffed and said nothing, but her maternal, officious stare momentarily forced Angelo back into his traumatic memory of Serenity, who had also stolen his money. He turned away so she wouldn't comment on his nervous eye twitch as she left, leaving a jar of soothing salve.

Angelo, alone for a minute as the doctor sat at his desk making notes, shuddered to recall his sojourn into the seedy district of Patpong as they visited several dens of iniquity out of curiosity. But the young girls behind the glass were alluring and ravishing. When he and his other buddy, Cristian, walked into the waiting room of one of the massage parlors, the elderly Thai hostess offered them a glass of spiked wine, smiled, and opened the drapes. Behind the large, glass window were a dozen or more very young, beautiful Thai girls in various poses of seductive nakedness.

Each young girl had a numbered sign around her neck. They smiled coyly, massaged their nubile breasts, and enticed Angelo and his friend with their spread legs to choose the lucky one.

"I picked number nine; my lucky number, Cristian. Who did you get?" he recalled asking his friend at that time. Cristian didn't answer; he didn't prefer girls. He abruptly left his buddy and walked across the street to search further for the young boys.

Angelo was suddenly brought back to reality as the nurse came back. It was the pain in his groin as the doctor felt his testicles. The nurse hovering overhead, frowning down at him just like his mother used to do when he was naughty, made him blink again.

He was nervous and frightened with that diagnosis but confessed, "Yes, Doctor, I heard of 'clap'. My friend and me, we went to the Patpong district for a massage. For my back. I hurt it lifting the heavy garbage pails in our ship's kitchens down below."

Dr. Carrera finished his notes and came back to his patient. He gently raised Angelo's testicles and then palpated his groin. "They're swollen, alright. Poor fellow. Painful, I see, and your inguinal glands are swollen, also. That discharge you have is most likely the venereal disease that I told you," he said, taking a swab of the penile discharge and putting the swab in the sterile bottle that the aide handed him.

"Curable, Doctor? Can I be cured? Will I lose my job here?" Angelo asked fearfully. "I need the money for my mother, who is a widow and suffering from arthritis. I should report that girl, shouldn't I?" he asked, holding his right eye to stop it from spasming.

The doctor shook his head as the nurse laughed at the idea. "Those girls in Patpong move daily so that they are not found again. They are poor children who make money to support their families living on the farms and villages in the north," the nurse explained as she labeled the bottle with Angelo's name.

The doctor washed his hands, dried them carefully, threw the towel in the garbage can, and looked about for his fedora. "Where did you put my fedora, nurse? Look, I'll have to quarantine you for now, but you'll be in port for a week, I'm told, to repair the rudders on your ship. Then we'll have the results and know for sure if it's gonorrhea. I'm sure it is, and we'll start you on penicillin in the meantime. You'll be better soon, son," the doctor said kindly.

The nurse told Angelo to dress and said, "Your hat, Doctor. I put your fedora on the back shelf for you," she said, handing him his hat.

Fujiyama watched Angelo dress but asked, "Fedora, Doctor Carrera? Why do you call it that?"

The doctor took his hat and lovingly brushed the brim clean. "Ah, interesting question. Back in the late 1800s, Sarah Bernhardt was playing in a drama on the New York stage. She acted the part of Princess Fedora Romazov, the heroine. Bernhardt was a cross-dresser, and preferred such a hat compared to the frilly, flowered hat she was first given. She called it "the fedora," and it became popular with the Italian mafia. It was very popular for Frank Sinatra, who had about a hundred and fifty of them. He wore a different fedora each time he was on stage."

"I remember it became fashionable for the women's rights movement. They adopted it later as their symbol," the nurse added smartly, looking at poor Angelo gently maneuvering his testicles into his underwear.

The doctor patted Angelo on the back before he sat down at his desk again and let Angelo get dressed. "You'll be fine, my boy. Don't worry. We'll get you back to work in no time so you can send money back to your sick mamma in your home country."

"You got more than a massage, young man. Was it worth it?" Fujiyama asked in a scolding manner as the doctor filled out the sick forms, blood work, and health insurance forms for time off.

Angelo was embarrassed to admit anything to this motherly figure. "No. She also stole my two hundred American dollars when she hung my pants up in the closet. And a package of condoms that my friend told me to buy. She was pretty, with a pretty name, Serenity ..." he said in hushed tones. He trailed off, embarrassed.

Fujiyama pointed her well-manicured finger at him again. "Clap, you have. Poor boy."

Angelo sighed with fear, blinking with his heart in his throat, as Fujiyama handed Angelo the bottle of penicillin capsules. "You are to take one when you get back to your room, and then one each day at the same time until they are finished," she said with a harsh tone.

She looked him in the eyes, shook her head in disdain, and then turned to dispose of the infected gloves in the sealed trash box for incineration.

"Thanks, miss," Angelo replied dutifully with head down, not looking at her. "I'll stay in my room as ordered. My friend will bring me my meals, as the doctor said." He watched the doctor leave to see another patient in the next-door examination room.

Fujiyama wasn't finished yet. "Serenity, young man, in English means tranquility, calmness, and peace. When you were with that girl named Serenity, it was definitely not a tranquil time for you, young man. Calmness and peace, you won't have for a while, and much more stress than you ever bargained for," Fujiyama said sternly, shaking her finger at him as she started to leave.

She stopped at the door and looked at him. "And get some tranquillizers for that eye twitch of yours. You're one of those Looney Tunes: a nervous Nelly. Blink, blink, blink," she said, blinking rudely with her right eye in ridicule. "And read all about safe sex online. Buy some condoms," she added, continuing her scolding the poor fellow.

Angelo only nodded and walked out, tenderly holding his groin. He felt relieved, in spite of the aide's brash warnings and the nervous humility of being scolded like his aunty used to do. He recalled the doctor's kind words about getting cured, helping his 'sick mamma,' and his continued ability to send her money on a regular basis.

GONORRHEA

Angelo was sexually active and involved with a prostitute. At the time, he didn't consider the consequences of a sexually transmitted disease (STD) or of being robbed.

Since he was in a foreign country, he also didn't think about being implicated in an anti-social, criminal activity, which prostitution may be. However it is presented, it is a serious crime in many countries. He was fortunate that the ship hadn't docked in some Middle Eastern countries or elsewhere, where, if caught, he could be found guilty and imprisoned for many years for having sexual relations outside of marriage.

He was lucky to only have lost money, and not his freedom, and only contracted gonorrhea, which can be cured.

Gonorrhea has become extremely prevalent once again. In the early 60s and 70s, it was cured by only one injection of penicillin. As time went on, penicillin and other antibiotics became prevalent, and thus eventually inefficient due to overuse.

"Clap," as the term was defined in Angelo's story, also became more prevalent due to promiscuity, the lack of protection by condoms, and carelessness in increased "acceptable" sexual activities in multiple different manners, interests, and pursuits.

STDs once again produce extreme anxiety and despair for the individual, but now also for communities. They have a serious drain on our medical system, cause grief and embarrassment to loved ones who could become infected, and could have serious, long-lasting effects with dire consequences for the individual.

This STD can infect men and women of all ages, regardless of culture, religion, or economic stature. It is spread through vaginal, oral, or anal sex, including the transmission to newborns during childbirth.

The only manner of avoidance of infection is by the use of condoms, being in a long-term, monogamous relationship (heterosexual or homosexual) with a partner who is free of the disease, or through abstinence. "Pulling out" during intercourse or believing that your one-time sex partner is free of gonorrhea is hopeless, and courts prolonged agony. Those who continue in such risky endeavors should see their physician and be tested for gonorrhea on an annual basis.

If the woman is pregnant and has a known case of the clap, then she must see her physician and be tested and treated. Otherwise, she will pass the infection on to her baby.

Gonorrhea is now again a very common infectious disease. According to the Center for Disease Control in the USA, in each year there are 700,000 new cases reported, with thousands still unreported. Sexually active teenagers have one of the highest rates of reported infections.

The common word 'clap,' as used to describe gonorrhea, came from the French word "*clapier*," meaning "hutch" (such as a rabbit hutch). Rabbits are viewed to be very sexually active. Over a hundred years ago, there was such an area in Paris known as "The Clapier," frequented by prostitutes and contained many brothels. Men and women who visited there and then had a discharge from the vagina or penis as a result of gonorrhea were then asked, "Hello, mon ami, have you been to The Clapier?" and they were then laughingly known to have had "the clap."

An infected person will know he or she has gonorrhea because it produces a burning sensation on urination and a colored, foul-smelling discharge. Many women could have pain in the lower pelvic area with disturbed menstruation. Men present with painful, swollen testicles. However, some women with gonorrhea may not have any symptoms known to them. It is at such a time that their sex partners are vulnerable, since those women are seemingly healthy.

Nevertheless, those women who are infected may complain only of burning urination, which can be a common malady for many women. Other, more clinical, symptoms include vaginal discharge, bleeding between periods, and sores in the pelvic area. Rectal and anal infections cause complaints in both sexes with bleeding, discharge, itching, soreness, and painful bowel evacuations.

If there is any such suggestion of infection, the person must see a physician. The doctor could take a swab of the discharge from the penis, vagina, rectum, or the throat, depending on the location of symptoms and a careful history of the type of sex involved. The doctor can then prescribe the appropriate medication, with instructions to avoid sexual activity for many days following active treatment. Treatment, if delayed, can be difficult since drug-resistant strains of the gonococcus bacteria are increasing.

Gonorrhea untreated or not responding to medication can cause serious health difficulties in both sexes. Women can develop chronic—that is, long-lasting—pelvic inflammatory disease, including infertility due to scarring and blockage of the fallopian tubes. Such tubes carry the ovum, the egg, from the ovaries to the uterus to hopefully meet the sperm to produce a baby. A woman, if pregnant, can have serious pregnancy complications or long-term pelvic/abdominal discomfort.

Men with untreated gonorrhea or failed treatment can have chronic pain in the testicles, swollen testicles, infertility, and, eventually, sterility. Both men and women can suffer from the spread of the infection into the bloodstream, thus affecting the joints and mobility. Finally, it may lower the overall immune system, causing the person to be more susceptible to other infections throughout the body or cancers.

Treatment can be successful if all therapy suggestions are closely followed.

Such STDs cause severe anxiety and despair for the infected person. Once again, talking about it with a counselor, a registered psychologist, in group therapy, or receiving medication and psychotherapy from a psychiatrist can be most helpful for the mental stress and ensuing psychiatric disorder.

JOSEPH THE BINNER

J oseph brushed the black engine oil from his shoulder as he picked himself off the grubby back lane in the Downtown Eastside. He watched the young tough who had pushed him down sneer and spit at him. The tough stole the twenty beer bottles from Joseph's Safeway cart that he had stolen from the grocery store last week. Joseph recognized the pock-faced drug addict with muscular arms laden with tattoos. He often saw Broderick at the Lutheran Church food bank every week.

"This is my territory, piss head. So, bugger off," Broderick growled as he again pushed Joseph against the dirty, brick wall lined with blue garbage bins. He kicked Joseph's Safeway cart into the oily puddle as he spat again. This time the nasal salvo was more accurate.

The older man's rain-soaked jean jacket was torn at the shoulder. His old, B.C. Lions t-shirt was worn out, as were his grubby sandals, both of different size and shape.

He wiped his face of saliva with his fingerless gloves, retrieved his cart, and gave the tough the finger as he walked away. He shook his left leg as he felt warm urine dribbling down into his old sandal.

He had wet himself when the heroin junkie attacked.

Joseph was only forty-six, but already an old man after hepatitis from alcohol, drugs, diabetes, and jail terms for theft. Both alcoholism and schizophrenia had robbed him of his youth. He was nearly bald, partly blind with cataracts, deaf in one ear after a fight, and all his teeth were loose or missing. His thin, wasted arms had trouble pulling his cart out of the way of a FedEx truck bearing down on him in the lane.

The back lane was very special, and sought after by all the binners. A therapist once told him that there were fourteen hundred bin divers in Vancouver collecting bottles, tin cans and other metal to recycle. The refuse supplemented their meager welfare income.

"This lane could give me enough cans, bottles, and metal to keep me until my disability check comes in next week," he mumbled to his fantasized friend, Renaldo, as he limped toward Burrard Street in Vancouver.

Joseph sat down on the corner curb at lunchtime and watched the office workers scurrying in and out of the pizza shop for a fast meal. He took his shirt off since the sun was high; it was going to be a hot day that late summer. He waved and called out to people walking by and stuck out a tin can.

"Fuck you too, man," he shouted out to the well-heeled young man who sneered at Joseph and told him to get a job. He wore an expensive, black, pin-striped suit and matching tie, but he told Joseph to piss off when he asked him for a hand-out.

A young woman, a tourist holding a street map, gave him a slice of her left-over pizza.

After an hour, Joseph got up, looked at his tin holding a few coins, scooped them into his pocket, and walked away, eating the cold slice. Pushing his Safeway cart, he looked up at the rows of newly-built, glitzy condos on his right. They were separated from the sleazy, vacant, wooden shops on his left bordering Pender Street. He hit the blue bins early that morning, hoping to beat the young crackheads who would push him aside.

He knew that the posh condos were full of young beer, gin, and juice drinkers, and after their Saturday night drunken parties, there would be lots of empties that Monday. If he was quick, he could make an easy forty dollars before the day was over.

He had another week to go before his next welfare check. The food bank at the Cathedral on Burrard was empty until the first of the month.

He left his empty cart in the doorway to his "hotel" and swore at the young crackhead sitting in the corner, waiting for his delivery of cocaine. He vacantly nodded to his desk manager as he walked up the four flights to his sparse, damp room. It had a filthy towel covering one dusty window and a mattress in the corner to sleep on.

As he walked in, he turned on his double hot plate, sold to him with the faulty switch that crackled and spewed a burning smell every time he turned it on. "It's a fire waiting to happen, Joe," Rachel, his next door neighbor, once told him. "You'll burn this place down and me in it," she added.

That hot plate just barely warmed up his can of Puppy Chow. It was mixed with cold water from the chipped sink tap and an out-dated can of beans that he'd gotten at half price. He was not happy to be living in the dilapidated "hotel" room that he called home because of his prying neighbor, Rachel. She was a hooker. He was sure of that—he often listened to her squeals of laughter through the paper-thin walls.

He inappropriately laughed out loud as he sat down to eat his lunch and then rolled himself a toke to smoke after his meal. "The joke is now on the bank manager," he whispered to Renaldo, his neighbor three rooms away.

His friend, Renaldo from Brazil, listened intently when Joseph told him that he was fired from his position as an assistant manager. "Yeah, piss on him. Only because I complained that all the customers were conspiring against the bank and stealing money from the ATMs and sending the money to Russia," he told his good buddy months ago.

Maybe that was what he said. Or was it a hallucination, something he heard when all alone, hungry, cold, and snorting coke? He wasn't sure.

"Thanks for believing me, Renaldo. Come, have some soup," he yelled out three times.

It was the pounding on the walls from next door telling him to shut up that really made him mad. "Piss off, you bitch," he yelled back. He threw his dish at Rachel's wall, and then furiously kicked at the wall.

He decided that he'd have to move again, since Rachel was sleeping with all the men in the rooming house. That included the corner bank manager, the morning radio weather announcer, and the desk clerk, whom he was sure was an FBI agent undercover and listening in to all his conversations.

It was that kind of similar suspicions and fiery temper, physical abuse, and accusing all his conspiring neighbors that caused his divorce from his wife of twenty years.

"I really miss my two children," he said to Renaldo as he cleaned up his mess on the floor. "Oh, thanks for reminding me, good buddy," he yelled out again as he opened his three bottles of tranquillizers from his meager cupboard. He swallowed the tablets with a gulp of dirty, stale water from the Puppy Chow can that he used as a glass.

He left his room after an hour of berating Rachel next door, checking the hallways for undercover cops. Unsteady from the side effects of his pills, he was looking forward to meeting his son, Theodore, in the café down the street.

"He's a good lad, and the only one who visits me, listens to me, and talks to me still," he yelled out to Rachel as he passed her door, kicking at it. He added, "He'll loan me a few dollars, he will. I hope he shows up."

Rachel yelled out through the door something about pissing off.

Joseph walked into the Stardust Café, but stopped at the door first. He cautiously looked around, hesitated, then finally took a few steps inside. *Those police buggers aren't here today. They won't get at me and make fun of my nose. No more photos of my big ears with their high-tech phones and mailing them to the President of America like they did before*, he thought to himself.

He sat down in the far corner. Far away from the RCMP women in plainclothes watching him and laughing about something he did last week on the corner. He was certain that they were the cops. He was sure of that. In disguise, they were. No doubt about that. He covered his ears with his toque.

Joseph felt more fearful when he saw Mabel, the waitress, smile at him as she refilled the coffee cups for the officers.

"Were they talking to you about me having sex with you last week?" he asked Mabel when she came to his table, pointing to the women.

Mabel just smiled, but ignored the question as she stood at his table carrying her coffee pot. She had heard those kind of delusions, false beliefs, before. "What will you have today, Joe?" the waitress asked kindly.

"Oh, just a pot of hot water, Mabel. The usual."

Mabel smiled, and looked at the owner. She waited until he gave her the okay.

She brought him a cup, a pot of boiling hot water, and a spoon and left. From behind the counter, she watched Joseph secretly bring out a teabag from his back pocket. He put the bag in the cup and poured the boiling water into the cup over it. He secreted the sugar cubes off the table and put them in his pockets.

He waited for his son, drumming his fingers on the table, sipping his tea and talking silently to himself and to Renaldo.

After an hour the tea was cold, the police women in disguise had left, and the café was filling up with tourists. They all sat far away from the strange-looking man.

His son didn't show up. He would have to move his meager belongings in the packsack by himself and sleep under the roof shelter of the grocery store across the street. It was safe there. Outside. Safer outside than hearing voices in his room and feeling nervous and suspicious of the undercover cops in that hotel.

It was time to go. Two punks in the corner were laughing at some jokes. He was sure the jokes were about him. They had to be high on crack. He was certain about that.

He saw Mabel coming with a plate. He got up. He didn't order anything, and he didn't have any money to pay her.

"Here, Joe. Here's some toast I made for you. It's okay, Joe. It's on the house. Don't worry yourself none," Mabel said, giving him the plate with four slices of buttered toast.

He grabbed the slices, wrapped them in the napkin from the table, stuffed them into his pocket, and started to leave.

Mabel stopped him and held his arm for a minute. "Wait up, Joe. Here's some jam the owner said you could have, also. You know, for your breakfast tomorrow," Mabel added.

Joseph didn't thank her and left in a hurry. He remembered that he had to keep his appointment the next day at 10 A.M. with his therapist at the community clinic. He'll have a decent sleep outside on the street for a change, away from that no-good, conniving hooker, Rachel, who was also a CIA agent.

"Doc Francis. She'll change my pills. She's like a good mother to me. I never had one after she left me as a kid. She'll give me some cash. She will. Always does," he shouted to Renaldo, who lived at the end of the hall, once he was back in his room.

He bundled up his meager clothes in the filthy pillowcase dotted with old specks of blood from his ear infection and gave Rachel the finger. He stuffed his empty Puppy Chow can, the toast, and the jam into his paper Safeway bag and left.

Joseph found his empty Safeway cart in the alley and shoved his meager belongings into the cart.

As he trudged along, he almost turned back. In the distance was the young tough with the tattooed body giving him the finger as he shoved a needle into his arm.

The tough shouted out for all to hear, "Smarten' up, dummy. Hey, weirdo man. Go see *One Flew over the Cuckoo's Nest*. You need a lobotomy, like that guy in that movie."

After sleeping soundly and feeling safe outside under the store canopy, Joseph did see Dr. Francis the next day at the community clinic. She listened patiently to his delusions and to his frightening hallucinations, both auditory and visual. She changed his meds and handed him the prescription.

"Listen, Joe. You take these regularly every day. You hear? They will take those frightening fears away and stop the voices. You'll feel better. I've got a nice, warm room for you now in a safe boarding house close by. It'll be much better for you. There are nice staff there who will look after you."

He was comfortable with Dr. Francis, so he sat back and listened carefully, nodding each time to her suggestions.

"I also had a chat with your son, Theodore. He called me to see how you were. Said he was sorry to have missed you at the restaurant."

Joseph sat up, excited. "He did? Said he was sorry? Missed his father?"

"Yes, Joe. Went to the wrong restaurant with your other son, Freddy. He said they will see you at your new digs and take you out once a week for lunch or dinner. You're lucky to have such a nice family, Joe. They are both very interested in you, despite your long-term illness, Joe."

Joseph was never happier to know that someone really cared about him. His eyes swelled up with tears when he thought of his sons thinking about him: really caring about and being considerate of their father. "I'll do what you say, doc. Follow your instructions and see my family often. I'm so happy that they know all about my condition, and that it's not a secret any longer," he said as he left, dabbing his tears away with the napkins that he had taken from the restaurant.

SCHIZOPHRENIA

The specific word, "Schizophrenia," is hardly a hundred years old, but the disorder has affected mankind from the beginning of time. The illness had been described by the early Egyptians, and the various symptoms and erratic behaviors have been well-defined in various ancient books. Greek and Roman literature recorded histories of individuals who had false beliefs and hallucinations with strange, anti-social behaviors.

The condition, in those times, was explained as being a fault of the heart, the uterus, blood poisons, or the result of demons. Evil possessions of the body was the most commonly accepted cause, and thus exorcising these demons (by bloodletting or letting out the "brain vapors" by drilling holes in the skull) was the cure. Many died from infections or brain trauma as a result.

The illness was first well described by Emil Kraepelin, a German physician, in around 1887. He used the words *"dementia praecox"* at first. He set out different categories of the illness and considered it to be solely a disease of the brain.

A Swiss psychiatrist, Eugen Bleuler, coined the term that we now use in 1911. He changed the name because it was not one of "dementia" in early life, as Kraepelin suggested. Both of these physicians described the various categories of the disorder in greater detail.

In the past few decades, the cause of schizophrenia has been associated with a more specific brain disorder, and is now considered to be biologically defined. The early medications, like chlorpromazines, in the 1950s were a first major step in treatment, but with research into the brain and biological efforts in treatment, the future for schizophrenia is now much brighter. Some researchers are studying the effects of diet as a cause, and may suggest other options for treatment.

"Schizophrenia" is the word presently used by physicians as a diagnosis of the illness. But in the past, it was considered to be an example of poor health that began at an early age, perhaps in the mid-to late-teens. Thus it was originally called "*dementia praecox*" many years ago: referring to a dementing condition that was precocious and starting from very early years.

Later, as it was studied by mental health physicians more thoroughly, it was concluded that it was a splitting of mind and body. In other words, it was a "schiz" (separation) of the body and of the mind, the mind being the "phrenium." Thus the name "schizophrenia."

This illness has disturbing consequences for both the individual affected and their family. The community is impacted if the individual lacks familial supports and does not receive the proper medical care. This becomes obvious in certain areas of the city, where such ill people sleep on the streets or take over the parks.

The diagnosis of this condition is dependent on several criteria, which must occur at the same time. One of these conditions is false beliefs, like suspicions that the person is being watched, talked about, recorded on camera, is being poisoned, their mind being read, or is somehow being thought about by others.

Another common element is hallucinations. Such hallucinations are dependent on the five senses. Thus, visual hallucinations are when the person sees things or people that others can't see; auditory hallucinations are hearing voices or noises. The other senses of olfactory (smell), tactile (touch), or gustatory (taste) are less common.

Other factors to make the diagnosis are disturbances at work, education, home, or socially. Some other factors are altered interpersonal relations, self-care, and failure to achieve generally in personal pursuits.

This illness must not be attributed to drugs or alcohol, although such addictions can precipitate the disorder. In young children with autism or a communication disorder, the diagnosis can be very difficult, but still requires the above-mentioned, ongoing, serious manifestations like delusions or hallucinations.

Schizophrenia may exist for a brief time as an acute disorder with subsequent remission, but then may relapse into multiple episodes or become chronic and longer-lasting. Mood disorders like depression or manic behavior may be present, requiring immediate care or hospitalization to prevent personal or social injury.

Males may be more aggressive if they are convinced that someone is a threat to them. Both sexes may also have difficulty in thinking appropriately, and usually they lack insight into their condition, instead blaming society, government, friends, or family for their malady.

The overall prevalence for schizophrenia in the world population appears to be approximately just under one percent. Some authorities report that there is a variation for culture, race, ethnicity, and by geographic origin (for immigrants and children of immigrants), but statistics are difficult to analyze.

The sex ratio differs across samples reported and across populations, since the diagnosis may not be well-recorded in some countries. Males seem to have a higher incidence of prolonged illness with a greater variation of symptoms. The peak onset for delusional and other severe symptoms for males occurs in the early-to mid-20s, and in the later 20s for females.

Depression is common in both sexes. Cognitive complaints, that is, memory and concentration, may persist long after remission of the major complaints and contributes to the ongoing disability for future education and employment. The course appears to be favorable in a quarter of patients, but the majority will require ongoing medical support, supervision from families and within the community, with added financial and medical assistance.

The risk factors appear to be environmental, with a higher incidence in some minority ethnic groups and in an urban setting. There is a strong contribution for genetic factors, with birth complications like oxygen depletion and greater paternal age being a factor. Much more investigation of specific factors is required.

Females have less aggression-associated symptomatology, but more emotional or depressive components.

Suicide attempts are higher for males with drug addictions, isolation, unemployment, and lack of overall supports. Cleanliness and obsessive features like tidiness and other obsessive-compulsive activities lead to a better prognosis.

Schizophrenia and other mental illnesses all have cognitive difficulties, that is, memory and concentration problems, which become worse with time. Thus, they forget to take their meds and have trouble problem-solving, with poor judgment and faulty social skills.

Treatment with a psychologist for cognitive remediation therapy to improve memory and concentration is most helpful. Also, the family and the public must be more aware of such cognitive disabilities and encourage therapy.

Prior to medication like chlorpromazine in the late 50s, the main form of treatment for schizophrenia, aggressive personalities, chronic depression, overwhelming anxiety states, and manic-depressive disorders was prefrontal lobotomy. That is, the cutting of the frontal lobes of the brain away from the rest of the central brain structure.

It was one of the earlier forms of treatment, long before tranquilizers were discovered. It was certainly very drastic, but with the multitude of such patients in mental institutions it became a treatment of choice, since it produced calmness and comfort for patients and staff alike. Still, how could such a drastic procedure evolve, advance, and be performed on tens of thousands of patients suffering from different forms of mental illness around the world?

It had been known for centuries that mentally disturbed persons were altered in thought and behavior if they had a crushing blow to the forehead. Such a blow could occur during battle, after a fall, or in some type of near-fatal accident. Furthermore, trephining, or drilling holes into the skull, was not uncommon in African culture and the early Mediterranean areas. Originally, the idea was to let out the evil and noxious vapors considered to be the cause of strange behaviors and ideas.

A neurologist in Lisbon, António Moniz, observed in 1935 that slicing the brain lobes at the front of the skull in violent and aggressive animals caused them to become docile and very manageable. He then offered this surgical procedure to a number of psychotic patients at the local lunatic asylum.

He drilled holes into the skull, just above the eyes, of the patient under anesthetic and inserted a scalpel to slice the frontal lobes away from the rest of the brain. The results were dramatic and curative, if the patients survived any potential ensuing infection or possible hemorrhage.

Moniz did other work in outlining the vascular system of the brain: he would inject a dye into the bloodstream and then take an x-ray of the brain. A year later, he received the Nobel Prize for his work.

Prefrontal lobotomy became the gold standard for the treatment of schizophrenia, but also for other mental disorders throughout the world. It was interrupted by the Second World War, but in North America over 20,000 patients were thus treated, and over 30,000 throughout Europe.

When the medication chlorpromazine, and then other similar chemicals, were introduced, this surgical procedure was no longer necessary. However, since the treatment required a surgical unit with specialized staff and a neurosurgeon (which was very expensive for hospitals), the icepick surgeon came on the scene.

A surgeon would start by sharpening an icepick. They would then mildly sedate the patient who sat, still awake, in a chair. The icepick would be deftly inserted just above the eyeball on one side. The bone just above the eyeball is very thin, and is located just below the frontal lobe.

Once the icepick was in place and a nurse was present to hold the patient still, they would quickly hammer the icepick with a wooden mallet up into the frontal lobe.

The patient felt a quick, sharp pain, but the surgeon would

then twist the icepick quickly and sever that frontal lobe. They then repeated the procedure on the other side. It was quick, and it saved the hospital a lot of money.

These icepick surgeons were much-sought-after due to their low cost; thousands were thus lobotomized. A number of well-known individuals in America fell to this practice, including John F. Kennedy's younger sister.

The only one who outlawed the procedure of prefrontal lobotomy was Joseph Stalin in Russia.

He said it was far too barbaric.

Patients and the families must remain optimistic as better treatments are now available. Community clinics, psychologists and psychiatrists are better equipped to help. Spiritual assistance is offered and our society is more accepting.

AMRITA'S OVERWHELMING FEARS

Amrita's mother opened her daughter's bedroom door at 7:30 in the morning and walked in to stir her sixteen-year-old daughter awake. She opened the curtains to let the sunshine in, opened the window wide, and walked to the bed, singing, "*Wake up sleepy head, wake up.*"

She gently pulled the blanket down from Amrita's shoulders and then the bed sheets wrapped about her head.

"Come, sweetie. You'll be late for school. Time to rise and shine, sleepy head. You've only got another two weeks of your final year at school, and then it's summer holidays; you will be off to the lake with all the family."

Amrita opened her eyes and pulled the covers back over her head. "Not going. No way. William will be there in my class today."

"William Pacino? The nice boy from across the street? He is in some of your classes, I heard, but so what?" Amrita's mother asked as she sat on the side of the bed and again pulled the covers back.

Amrita waited. She was taking in short, shallow breaths, and her mother could see the beads of sweat forming on her head. "

So, he pushed me into the pool when we all went swimming at the gym two days ago. I almost drowned. I couldn't breathe. I was going to die," she answered, gasping for breath. She took her mother's hand and held it tight.

Her mother felt that hand tremble, clammy and wet from sweat. "Here, let me take your pulse. Maybe you've got a fever," she said, checking her watch as she counted the beats. "It's fast, but you're not coughing, and your forehead isn't hot. Just clammy, you poor dear."

"Promise me that you won't make me go swimming at the gym again, Mom. When I think of almost drowning, my heart starts to race and I can't think or breathe; I'm going to freak out again. He'll be there again."

"Okay, dear. Okay. No need to go to the gym. I promise. But he is such a nice boy."

Amrita sat up in bed and grasped her mother's hand again. "You promise, Mom. You promise? Promise?" she pleaded and then added, "Not nice, Mom. Not nice. He called father a 'curry-muncher' and a 'Paki with a big beard that looks like Santa Claus.' He did it in front of all my friends, he did, after calling me 'curry-girl.'"

"Oh, my dear. That's not nice. Is that what's gotten you so nervous?"

Amrita became more agitated. Her head shook as she tried to nod affirmative.

Her mother recalled that her daughter was also nervous of heights. Two years ago, she had taken her up on the Seattle Space Needle for a holiday weekend of shopping. She had an acute asthmatic attack and fainted, and then threw up in the elevator as they descended.

She also almost fainted again when she saw the needle that the family doctor brought out. It was last year, when Amrita's mother took her for her pneumonia shot.

Her mother hesitated for a minute. "Sweetie, your dad asked me if you had a swig out of his brandy bottle last night, when we went out to the movies?"

Amrita only nodded but turned away, embarrassed. "My stomach was upset. I had the chills, and I couldn't breathe. Don't tell Dad," she pleaded.

She wasn't going to tell her parents about buying marijuana from her older brother, Baldev. He'd told her it would calm her down last month when she went to his room next door.

"You got all uptight and freaked out after watching that movie, 'Alien,' on that small TV set in your room, Amrita," Baldev said, chastising his younger sister.

Amrita's mother helped her daughter out of bed.

"I'll be all right now that we talked, Mom. I'll go to school today and on Monday after this weekend, Mom. I want to practice my guitar and finish that song for our little nephew."

As Amrita got up and dressed, she said, "My grade eleven home teacher said I could see the school counselor. She saw me retching, and I confided in her,"

Amrita's mother felt relieved and left her daughter to get dressed. "Okay, dear. Little Ahmed, your cousin, will like listening to the children's songs that you have composed. As to the school counselor, promise me you'll do that; that's a good idea. I met the counselor, Fredericka, at the parent/teacher meeting last month. She seemed nice. But your father said that you have to regain your composure: calm down and get it together once and for all, dear."

Amrita feared her father's wrath. Where would she go if she didn't 'get it together,' she wondered?

She shuddered and held her breath again, but then took slow, deep breaths to calm herself. She got dressed and waited until she heard her mother had gone down the hallway. She quickly went to her bookcase and moved away one of her large textbooks.

She reared back as a very small, black spider scurried across the bookcase and disappeared into the open window.

"Bad luck. Black spider. I hate bugs and spiders." She almost yelled out loud, but put her hand over her mouth, fearing her mother would hear and come back to scold her.

"And forget about the lake, mother. Full of ants, bugs, snakes, and black spiders there," she whispered to herself. She would tell her mother about that later.

Taking in some deep breaths and slamming the window tight, she reached into the bookcase and pulled out a small, plastic bag. "Damn. It's empty," she wailed and threw the bag back into the bookcase.

She heard Baldev talking to his girlfriend on his cellphone next door. "Thank Christ he's home just before the weekend," she said. She looked out her door to hear her mother in the kitchen and her father outside mowing the grass.

Amrita checked her purse and took out two twenties. She tiptoed to Baldev's door, quietly rapped, and heard him yell to enter. He was off the phone and pulling on his jeans.

"Baldev you've got some of that weed?" she pleaded. She flashed the money and handed it to him.

Baldev looked at her. She was wide-eyed and scratched at the rash on her neck. She was breathless and pale, ready to faint. "Come—sit down before you fall down, little sister."

She sat down on his bed, white as a sheet. "I'm choking, Baldev. My stomach is upset, and I'm going to throw up, Baldev. Sell me some, please. It will calm me down," she implored, holding her gut, gagging.

Baldev quickly brought her his wastepaper basket in case she vomited all over his bed. "What's going on, little sister?"

"It's that William and his buddies. They're mean, and I almost drowned when he pushed me in the water at the gym. His buds held me down, laughing. They said that I had a funny name and my nose was too big." She retched.

Baldev felt sorry for his sister as she held his wastebasket in front of her. "You're suffering from a phobia, little sister. I read about that in my psychology class, last year before I got into law school."

Amrita was pacing up and down, impatient as he rolled her a toke. She grabbed it out of his hand and brought out a lighter from her pocket. He sat back and watched her inhale deeply.

After a few minutes, she had calmed down.

"Father has got tickets for us on Air India to visit his mother in Delhi. She's dying of bowel cancer. This summer: July. Going to be hot in Delhi," Baldev explained as he opened the window and waved the smoke out.

Amrita almost choked on her joint. She gagged as she got up and took a breath of fresh air at the window. "No way, Baldev. No way am I flying, grandmother or not. You'll have to knock me out first to get me on that flight. Not me," she howled as she walked about his room. She pushed her brother back and forcefully grabbed his stock of weed. She ran out, crying.

"Poor girl. 'Aerophobia' that lecturer called it," Baldev recalled to himself as he closed his window. His father shouted something from below about not smoking in the house.

Amrita stayed at home and refused to go to school that Friday, in spite of her mother's pleadings. She spent most of her time on her cellphone: on Facebook, playing video games, and smoking her cannabis.

Amrita locked herself in her room all weekend, smoking and strumming on her guitar. She refused to eat. That Monday, she complained of the stomach flu. When she saw the same spider crawl across her closed window, she threw up into her wastepaper box.

Her mother told her father about her phobias, so he finally called their family doctor.

The doctor, who was a friend of the family, made a house call that Saturday when her father called urgently. Amrita let him come up to her room.

Dr. Mustafa sat on her bed and listened patiently to her phobias. After a time, he told her she was phobic and assured her that she would be better with counseling. He said he would also write out a prescription for a mild sedative for her as he left.

He gently escorted Amrita downstairs to be with the family.

"We'll get her an appointment with a good therapist, a psychiatrist," he told the parents as he sat and had a cup of green tea in their living room downstairs. He wrote out a prescription for a calming tranquillizer and a sedative at bedtime and gave it to her father.

Dr. Mustafa tried to reassure Amrita that her situation was not unusual. "My little niece, Claudia, had a similar fear, Amrita, when she was a small child. Someone pushed her into a swimming pool at a neighbor's pool party. She was quickly rescued, but thereafter she refused to go with her father, my brother, in their boat at the lake. She is still scared of open water, but she is slowly getting better. You will get better too, my dear."

Amrita's brother joined the family and the doctor in the kitchen for some samosas and looked at his sister. "Listen up, sister.

I don't want my friends knowing you're seeing a counselor. It's embarrassing for me. Especially if I get into law school; not good for my reputation. I want all this to be kept in the family: not out with my friends, or even at your school." He pointed his finger at his sister and walked out.

Amrita's mother, embarrassed by her son's tirade, made more tea and they sat around the kitchen table, eating samosas and tasty bits of chicken cooked in coconut curry.

Amrita calmed down, pale but silent, as the doctor spoke to her father. "I listened to the track of her singing on her guitar. She has a real knack of producing songs for little children, Mr. Assami. I especially loved that one called, "The Wacky Wabbit Chasing Mister Daffy Duck in the Farmyard."

He looked at Amrita. "I'll buy it when you've finished it, Amrita. For my six-year-old son. He loves 'wabbits.' Has a wee, white, 'wacky wabbit' as a pet," he said, laughing. He left nibbling on a samosa.

PHOBIC DISORDERS

A phobia is simply an overwhelming fear, usually of a very specific object or situation, as in the above story with Amrita. Unfortunately, it did not only affect this young girl, but it also dearly affected her brother and her parents. Her illness had an effect on her social welfare, her education, and could have an impact on her future employment. Phobias can be very inhibiting, as it was for Amrita.

Some examples of phobias are fear of flying, heights, animals, pests, or, as Amrita complained, of snakes, spiders, needles, and of drowning. The last has a cause: her head was held underwater by her classmates, combined with the humiliation of her family culture.

The situation immediately produces overwhelming anxiety and a fear of death. It doesn't make sense to others, and the anxiety is out of proportion to the actual danger. The event is immediately avoided in order to protect that person from danger.

The illness causes overwhelming distress and disability with impaired social, occupational, and many other areas of daily functioning.

Phobic disorder is different from other mental disorders like an ongoing anxiety disorder, panic disorder, post-traumatic stress disorder, or obsessive-compulsive disorder that all have an anxiety component to them. It is common to have multiple specific phobias, as Amrita demonstrated.

The phobia is defined by the objects or events specified (e.g. of snakes, heights, injections, etc.). The major feature is overwhelming anxiety that becomes incapacitating. However, it is generally brief and specifically related to the fearful object or situation. It can be reduced with avoidance of the object or with a tranquillizer.

It is different from a stress or "normal" anxiety following transient fears common to everyone periodically. Characteristically, it occurs only when confronted with the specific object or stimulus. The degree of fear expressed or the anxiety experienced is immediate and disabling. It usually occurs in the presence of others, and depends on the duration of exposure and the extent of the threat. Avoidance is a paramount feature, which precludes attending or being involved in situations where the fearful object may be encountered, such as elevators, swimming pools, heights, or enclosed areas like airplanes.

Individuals with phobias have anticipation anxiety when thinking or intending to be involved in areas where there might be a phobic stimulus. This could occur in airports, gardens where pests might lurk, forests and bushes where animals might live, or attending school where Amrita, in the above fictionalized story, was humiliated.

The prevalence rate in North America is approximately close to 10%, and females appear to have the double rate over males. A traumatic event usually precipitates the phobia, like being attacked, injured, stuck in an elevator, sexually abused, or observing others going through severe trauma.

Specific phobias often develop in early childhood. They usually express their phobic anxiety by crying, having tantrums, being aggressive, freezing, or clinging. They may not be able to express the cause or understand the reason for their avoidance.

Ongoing phobias must be understood by the parents of that child and assessed depending on the duration of the fear and the extent of the avoidance.

Specific phobias that are confined to only one object or situation in the older population is relatively rare, but it is common for the elderly to develop certain other general fears. Such fears can be overwhelming, and cause the person to avoid such areas or situations.

For example, the fear of falling down will prevent older persons from using the stairs or going out for a walk. Medical cardiac issues, obesity, breathing problems, or arthritic pains will produce a phobic avoidance of any movement, exercise, or social interaction. The pain, cardiac flutter, or asthmatic attack becomes crushing, embarrassing, and disabling.

There are certain risk factors that may encourage the development of a phobic disorder. Severe introversion and personality inhibitions, plus parental overprotectiveness, parental loss or separation, and abuse of various types create a higher risk of predisposition.

Naturally, the experience of other traumatic encounters in the past will add to future disability. Individuals with a first degree relative, such as a mother or father, who are phobic can develop the same phobia. You may have seen a parent grip their child's hand tightly as they get into an elevator and say, "Now dear, don't worry. There is nothing to be frightened of."

Persons with phobias have social and personal problems in coping, similar to others with a variety of mental disorders. Those with multiple phobias have much greater difficulties in managing their lifestyle.

All patients, young and old, need to be evaluated for possible medical reasons for the cause of the fear or anxiety associated with a phobic disorder. For example, feeling dizzy or fainting may be due to a very low blood sugar or diabetes.

Other urgent evaluations are necessary for those with cardiac abnormalities like irregular heartbeat or flutters, adrenal problems (high adrenaline levels causing tremors), high blood pressure, thyroid disorders, cancers, Parkinson's, various medications, sexually transmitted diseases, and the addiction to drugs or alcohol.

Phobic disorders respond very well to early evaluation and treatment. A physical examination is essential to rule out possible medical reasons. Psychotherapy counseling by a registered therapist is most beneficial. Group therapy is comforting and supportive, as is spiritual counseling, and the individual can become a mentor to others.

A family physician can prescribe essential medication or suggest yoga, meditation, acupuncture, or other modalities. A psychiatrist may be aware of better, more effective, medication and have the time to include family or couples therapy.

Once again, it is most helpful to talk about this illness openly with friends, family, or in group situations. This and other such mental concerns are now more frequently discussed in the newspapers, radio, TV, and within social media. People like Amrita's brother are no longer embarrassed to talk about this. It is no longer "hush-hush."

SYPHILITIC CARMELITA

Carmelita still felt dizzy and confused from the anesthetic. She flinched from the pain and whimpered softly as the doctor stitched up her birth canal after the delivery of her newborn. Now that she was in the hospital in America, she felt safe. But she was still nervous and fearful as to her, and her newborn son's, future. She tried to hide the red rash on her face caused by her anxiety when the nursing staff spoke to her, but she was unsuccessful.

As she lay there with her legs still up in the stirrups, she wondered where the rest of her small, ragged group was, and if they might be hiding in the bushes. They had dragged her across the border into California in the middle of the night and then had scattered in fear. She wasn't sure what happened to her boyfriend, Manuelito, when he was taken away by the border guards.

She remembered him threatening her whenever she picked at her face when she was so anxious. "Stop poking at your cheeks with your fingers, or I'll give you a poke in the face with my fist," were his last words when he'd finished having his way with her in the Mexican fields and left her all alone.

She could feel the doctor down there somewhere, poking around, but she couldn't see him. Waiting patiently for the nurse to bring in her baby boy took an eternity and not seeing the young doctor or knowing what he was doing down there made her blush. After all, being so nakedly exposed in front of a young, handsome man would never be allowed in her small village in northern Guatemala.

Confused, embarrassed, and still drowsy from the bronchitis that she'd gotten from the cold nights in the hills of Mexico, plus the intramuscular needle in her arm to calm her down, she lapsed in and out of consciousness.

But it was that final, weary trek across Mexico and the rush across the border with her boyfriend, Manuelito, that had exhausted her. Plus his demands every night in the rotting sleeping bag in the hills. Then the pregnancy. It was all too much for the young woman and her frail body.

The doctor, a young man from Bolivia in his fourth and final year as a resident in obstetrics, finally looked up beyond the drape covering his patient. He told the nurse to give her more Demerol in the intravenous tube to help her with the pain.

"Sorry, missus, but I had to make the cut, the episiotomy, in the vaginal wall during the delivery. Your baby's head would have torn you badly," the young obstetrics resident, Juan Carlos, said kindly, partially in Spanish so she could understand fully.

She murmured something.

He then said, "Do you understand what I am saying, missus? Did you hear me? Another doctor, a psychiatrist named Dr. Milhouse, will see you in the morning to help you with your severe depression, missus." After a pause, he added, "and another specialist for the infection."

Carmelita roused briefly after what seemed like forever. She felt her heart thump against her breast bone with her nervousness. Yes, she did understand what the doctor said, apart from the infection. "Yes, I hear you, but I am no missus. No missus, Doctor," she explained as the nurse increased the amount of Demerol through the IV. She drifted off into oblivion once more.

Once again, she was somewhere in the mountains: frightened, hungry, cold, dehydrated, coughing up specks of blood, and in agony from blistered toes and aching hips. It was after trekking over dirty fields, climbing hills, and walking through stretches of desert and cold ditches full of water that caused her to lose two fingertips to the frostbite in the cold nights. She was then several months pregnant and could hardly keep up with the others.

She could always smell him, unwashed after so many months of sweat and grime, sleeping next to her and demanding that she roll over toward him all night. But in the mornings, he was beside her, urging and pushing her and the other forty seeking freedom along the gritty paths.

The weather had finally cleared as they came close to California, but her pains were becoming more frequent, and she feared her water would break before they crossed the river and the border into America.

"Come quickly, Carmelita. We are into America now, and I was told that San Diego has a hospital. It is not far," Juanita, an older woman who cared for her with the pregnancy, had yelled at her last week.

It was Manuelito who pushed and pulled her along the slippery, muddy slope into the outskirts of the small town across the border. And then he said he would leave her. As he left her he whispered, "Now you are a wetback. Be careful of the young gringos in America who would want you in their bed and use you." Then he disappeared.

It was the pain of the last suture being inserted that woke her up and forced her back to reality. She shook her head to clear it of the horrific dream and traumatic memories as another nurse brought in her new baby boy.

Megan, an Irish nurse with flaming red hair and bright green eyes, laid him down in her outstretched arms next to her left breast. She accepted him, and he immediately snuggled in close to her breast to feed.

She wanted so much to see his beautiful face: to see if he had her father's eyes, his nose and dark hair. Looking down at him, she smiled, since he did have a mass of dark hair. She waited; she was sure he was hungry, and her breasts were bloated.

Carmelita was relieved that the doctor had finished. Her legs were brought down, and she was covered in a warm electric blanket.

The young doctor, Juan Carlos, a close friend of Dr. Milhouse, came to her side and smiled at the tender scene. But he was ominously silent. He only nodded and whispered something to one of the other obstetrical nurses.

Carmelita couldn't hear what he said, but she saw the worried look on his face with the hushed tone as he spoke.

More awake as her baby suckled, she marveled at the clean, white, sterile walls, nurses in blue uniforms scurrying about, and inhaled the pungent anesthetic odors flooding the room.

Carmelita looked up at the doctor who took her hand and kindly said, "It is good that you are in your middle twenties, Carmelita. Your labor was uncomplicated."

Carmelita only nodded. She feared telling him the truth, in case she be sent back to her own country; she had lied about her age to the border guards.

"I am no missus, Doctor," was all she said again, but didn't reveal that she was only sixteen. With this fear, she tried hard not to scratch at the marks left on her face from her childhood chicken pox infection and the recent rash.

Another nurse, in a blue uniform, came to her side. "Ah … a beautiful baby you have now. But I'm sorry to tell you that he has an infection. He will be fine. Don't you worry now—at all. I will help you, also with the English," the nurse, wearing a head shawl, spoke in broken Arabic to her patient. She soothed her brow with a cool towel.

It was only after the baby had suckled briefly that he reared back, coughed, and spluttered as warm milk gushed out of the distorted cavity where his nose should be.

Carmelita pushed him away and shouted out in alarmed, hesitant English. "My baby, my boy; he is not my baby, nurse. Look, look," she yelled in revulsion, and added, crying, "He has not a nose; what have you done to his nose? My father had a fine nose, a fine nose. This one has none."

This was when the nurse, with cellphone in hand, immediately called the obstetrical consultant. She ever-so-gently took the little boy from her patient's outstretched quivering hands, swaddled him back into a warm blanket, and took him away just as the older consultant walked in.

Carmelita immediately began talking in a gibberish of Spanish and English, crying, wailing, and shaking uncontrollably as Dr. Bernard Gabreski stood at her side. "Will he be well? My father was a strong, healthy man: a mayor in our town, there in the village. He lived to an old age … with a fine, handsome nose. I can't remember how old," she babbled in hesitant English, in shock at the sight of her baby boy.

The doctor nodded to the nurse as she gave the baby to another to take away. The doctor told the nurse to prepare a tranquillizer as he scanned her admission chart. "I am sorry to tell you, Mrs. Toscano, that your baby has congenital syphilis: an infection. His nose is deformed; as we call it, a saddle nose. There is no bridge to his nose, and we fear that he may be blind. He has, also, a bad rash on his buttocks and a slight fever, as do you. Do you understand me, Mrs. Toscano? Do you understand what I am trying to explain, missus?"

Carmelita winced as the nurse gently inserted the intramuscular needle into the deltoid muscle in her shoulder. It was the calming, soothing voice of the older gentleman, with a mustache like her father's, that calmed her somewhat, rather than the sedative that would soon put her to sleep.

The doctor scanned her chart again. "It says here that you are twenty-eight years old, missus. Have you had other pregnancies?"

She hesitated. Would he send her back to Guatemala? "No. No," she lied. She wasn't going to be truthful and tell him that she was only sixteen.

"Very well, missus. You can stay here in the hospital while we do some tests."

"Missus, I am not. Carmelita is me, and she is not married. Manuelito Toscana: it was he who saved me when the truck turned over. It was in the ditches as we escaped from Guatemala to be with my uncle here in America. Somewhere. Manuelito is not husband. He hated my village, and helped me and others to walk into your country, here."

"Slowly. Slow down, lady. You are getting very anxious, and your face is all red from a rash. We will help you," the nurse said to calm her down.

"No, I ... I ... don't understand ... I want to see my uncle ...

my uncle; call him to come to me. A saddle? Like on a horse? A fever … rash … I … don't …" She drifted off into a deep, deep sleep.

Carmelita met with the Arab nurse and Dr. Juan Carlos the next day in the recovery ward. The two of them slowly and carefully explained that her baby, not yet named, had congenital syphilis and a bad heart.

"The spirochete bacteria have been passed onto your baby through your placenta and birth canal," the nurse explained, wiping her patient's tears aside.

Carmelita listened, but didn't understand.

The doctors surmised that she had contracted this dreaded disease from her friend, her "husband" Manuelito, who also had many "wives" in Ecuador and Guatemala, according to the police. He was in jail, under guard, and was wanted throughout Central America for assault, rape, robbery, and drug dealing. He was to be deported.

Carmelita wept uncontrollably and told the nurse her sad story. "I knew he had a bad stink from below, from his peepee, when we met some years ago," she explained as she cried. "But he said it was nothing after every time he did it with me. I needed him, as I had no one … so we were in the same bed always. Always."

Dr. Juan Carlos and the consultant were at Carmelita's bedside that next day, anxious about her bronchitis and her deep depression after the news of her syphilis and her child's terminal illness.

"You will have to do more blood work on her again, and take some genital swabs for syphilis," Dr. Gabreski said, motioning to his sleeping patient after she was further sedated.

He added, "And tell the guards at the prison detention center with Manuelito that if he is still there he, and all the other women in that group that he ushered across, are to be assessed for syphilis. He most likely had sex with most of them, too, back in their countries or here. He was the leader of that group. Made money off them and their families, and most likely sex was part of the deal."

Juan Carlos nodded in agreement. "Manuelito is still there, on the other prison ward with pneumonia. He has symptoms of syphilis, but has been kept under guard after they found his suitcase full of fentanyl and cocaine," he said as he walked away with his mentor.

He had never seen the venereal disease before clinically, but had read about its surging prevalence in medical journals. He had read that syphilis was immune to penicillin now, and was rampant throughout America and elsewhere as a sexually transmitted disease.

"And put her, and maybe Manuelito, on a suicidal watch," Dr. Gabreski ordered as they both walked out. "Until that shrink, Milhouse, sees them and gets them off my wards. Transfer them into his psych ward. I don't want them here, jumping out the windows. They all must be nuts to make that long trek," he said pointedly to his intern.

Juan Carlos flinched at such biased and unprofessional sarcasm coming from his mentor, but he had heard that kind of talk before. He would make sure that Carmelita had proper, close monitoring, but in a warm, safe surrounding: like the psych ward in this hospital.

He had spent a month on that psych ward as part of his training. He knew that the nursing staff and the psychiatrists would be kind to Carmelita and help in her recovery after the severe trauma that she'd gone through with Manuelito, and now with her newborn baby.

Carmelita was quickly transferred to the psych ward for the treatment of her severe postpartum depression. Her baby died a week after birth from his inability to eat and a congenital syphilitic heart condition, but she was making a good recovery from her syphilis infection with antibiotics.

Her anxiety and posttraumatic stress of being abused by Manuelito responded well to therapy. Her guilt of consenting to him during all those nights abated when she learned that he was sent to prison for ten years for transporting drugs, and would soon be deported back to his home country of Venezuela for imprisonment.

She cautioned Dr. Juan Carlos about her uncle, who was living in San Diego and soon to visit her. "No one is to know about my baby son or that infection given to me. Not my uncle or anyone. Do you promise?"

Juan Carlos knew that it would be an embarrassment to her family back home. He nodded. "I promise; it will be a confidential hospital record."

One day, when Juan Carlos visited Carmelita on the psych ward and sat having lunch with her and talking about their future together, she asked, "That bad man said to me that now I was a wetback. To be careful also of the gringos. What are those words?"

Juan Carlos smiled and held her hand warmly. "When people from Central America and Mexico crossed the border into America, some swam across the Rio Grande river, which is part of the border. They were soaking wet, Carmelita."

"Aha, they were wet. And so 'wetbacks.' But gringos?"

"Yes. When the Americans fought the Mexicans in that war many years ago, they went all the way down to Mexico City. The Mexicans hated that army. Those soldiers were all dressed in green uniforms in those days. The Mexicans would see them on their streets and shout out over and over again: Green go. Green go. Green go … home."

The light bulb came on for Carmelita as she understood. "Aha … so it became the gringos." She laughed as she finished her tea.

The young intern from Bolivia, Juan Carlos, helped Carmelita

LAWRENCE E. MATRICK M.D.

find a nice, clean rental after her discharge. He planned to marry her soon, so she could remain in America as his wife. He hadn't told her yet that she wouldn't be able to have any more children. He knew from her medical investigations that her fallopian tubes were scarred from her syphilitic   infection. Any eggs that she would produce wouldn't be able to travel down the blocked tubes to her womb.

As a physician, he knew of some options in the future with his sperm and her eggs.

However, Carmelita had already heard from Juan Carlos's older sister, Liotta, who visited frequently, that she would rent out her womb at a price for impregnation with Carmelita's eggs and Juan Carlos' sperm. It would be through in vitro fertilization when they were ready to do so, she said.

SYPHILIS

A recent newspaper article reported that the province of Manitoba in Canada had multiple cases of confirmed syphilis. Also, what was even more astounding was that many babies were born in that province with congenital syphilis.

"In BC alone there are 919 reported cases of syphilis in 2018, representing the highest number of cases in 30 years. The BC provincial health officer declared a syphilis outbreak in July 2019 and guidelines are now in place for enhanced screening for syphilis in pregnancy as of September 2019." (BC Medical Journal, October 2019)

According to the Center for Disease Control, over 50,000 cases of syphilis were reported in America alone just over 5 years ago. In the United States, there has been a sharp increase of babies similarly borne with the dreaded disease. This disease is called congenital syphilis: that is, a disease passed on to the baby of an infected mother with syphilis.

Syphilis infection is highest in both sexes between the ages of 20 to 24.

Other recent statistics are that sexually transmitted diseases (STDs) among the elderly are a common and growing problem. Between 2007 and 2011, STDs among Americans sixty-five and older increased by 31%, and syphilis especially by 52%. HIV in the elderly is now more prevalent.

The reasons are multiple. Older men are using erectile disorder medication, and older women who are menopausal won't get pregnant if a condom isn't used. Online dating is common, and sexual histories and infections are not discussed openly in such relationships. Finally, as people age, their immune systems weaken, making them more susceptible to STDs.

Infections among women fifteen to forty-nine years old increased by nearly 40% according to recent reports.

The disease has distressing consequences for both sexes, causing overwhelming anxiety and despair for the infected individual with significant complications on intimate relationships. It now has a serious impact on the medical system, as outlined in the above fictionalized story with Carmelita's medical needs.

Syphilis, like gonorrhea, is a sexually transmitted disease that was quickly treated with penicillin many years ago. However, like gonorrhea and other sexually transmitted diseases, this is no longer the case because of the overuse of antibiotics through the years. These bacteria have the ability to change and become immune to treatment.

Syphilis commonly has a number of different stages as it progresses in the infected body. Both men and women of all ages can become infected.

A person with primary syphilis has one or multiple sores around the original site of infection. That is around the penis, the vagina or surrounding area, the anus, or around the mouth. Such sores may be painless, in pustule form, or firm and round.

As the infection spreads, secondary syphilis is diagnosed with skin rashes, fevers, and painful, swollen lymph glands. Both the primary and secondary types may easily be disregarded as minimal by the infected person, go unnoticed, or be grossly misdiagnosed.

In the third, or latent, stage there may not be any complaints, and the disease may be totally disregarded by the individual or by the physician. In this final tertiary stage, it may be too late for full recovery.

Syphilis produces severe medical disorders and requires full evaluation, blood tests, and careful history. The spirochete, a bacteria that under the microscope looks like a corkscrew, has at this point invaded the bloodstream and infected the spinal cord and brain. Paralysis and insanity follows, and death may not be far off.

This last stage is referred to as General Paresis of the Insane. The unfortunate person with GPI suffers from weakness in all limbs due to paralysis of the nerves. They also fall into psychosis, insanity due to cerebral atrophy of the brain. It is a stage far too late for treatment, other than supportive care prior to death. The mental hospitals had many such men and women with GPI prior to antibiotics.

Édouard Manet, the well-known French artist and painter, succumbed to complications of the fatal illness and died in his early 50s.

There are a few other well-known historical personalities who succumbed to the dreaded disease, such as Theo van Gogh (brother of Vincent), Al Capone (the Mafia boss), Vladimir Lenin of Russia (after his time in France), Oscar Wilde, and Henry VIII of England. Some of these were never fully diagnosed due to the lack of laboratory analysis and confirmation in those days, but they had the classical symptoms of syphilis.

The only way to avoid this dreaded disease is to reject any sexual dalliance with an infected person or to remain in a long-term, committed, monogamous relationship. If there is any concern or doubt, then each partner should be examined, evaluated, and tested for syphilis. Also, if in doubt then the use of latex condoms during intercourse, vaginal or anal, is essential. Oral sex is next to impossible for prevention as sores may occur in areas not visible and oral cancer may develop.

Many medical authorities suggest that pregnant women should be tested for syphilis. If there is any concern, then a medical consultation is essential.

Those who are active with multiple partners, male or female, should be tested. Positive tests require immediate treatment. Sores may be painless and may disappear, but treatment is still required. Rashes usually occur on the palms of the hands or soles of the feet.

Other vague symptoms may be a slight fever, fatigue, swollen lymph glands in the inguinal/pelvic area, sore throat, muscle aches, visual eye changes, and, eventually, weight loss.

A simple blood test will diagnose syphilis, or a swab from a sore is diagnostic. The correct antibiotic (or multiple antibiotics) can be curative.

A person can be reinfected after treatment and follow-up evaluation needed. The sex partner may be infected since sores may not be obvious and the bacteria in the sores may still be in the vagina, under the foreskin, on the penis, around the anus, or in the mouth.

Carmelita in the earlier fiction story was very courageous but unaware that she had syphilis, contracted from Manuelito, who had multiple sex partners. She passed the spirochete bacteria that causes syphilis onto her baby. Her poor, innocent baby was then born with congenital syphilis. It has been reported that there has been a sharp increase of such babies born with syphilis in the United States and Canada.

Congenital syphilis is the disease that develops when the mother with syphilis passes the infection to her baby during pregnancy. Such an infection in the mother can cause a miscarriage, a stillbirth—that is, a baby born dead—or a premature birth—a baby born too early and not fully developed. The baby may be born but with very low birth weight or die soon after birth.

Those babies who are born may have bones that are deformed, a low blood cell count, or jaundice (yellow skin or eyes). A large abdomen due to an enlarged liver or spleen may occur. Finally, meningitis, an infected brain, is a potential complication, with rashes, a saddle nose, or other facial malformation. If the brain is infected, then severe damage including paralysis, blindness, and deafness may result.

Such a newborn may not show any of the above symptoms for some time following birth. The unfortunate complications may be dormant for weeks or months, and then require immediate treatment on evaluation. Such babies have a poor prognosis (medical outcome), and suffer dearly later if untreated or are unresponsive to treatment.

Public health professionals are very concerned about the rapid spread of syphilis and congenital syphilis in newborns. The incidence of this disease is growing rapidly. Treatment is possible if diagnosed early in the woman or her baby, and regular follow-up is essential.

Hospitalization may be necessary for a spinal tap to evaluate if the bacteria are in the spinal fluid or in the brain. It is recommended that testing for syphilis occurs early on in a pregnancy during the prenatal visit.

Again, if there is any doubt, then the woman must be examined with blood testing, a complete history, and a thorough physical. Her partner, or partners, must also be tested.

If treated, then a woman or man can again be infected with syphilis if the proper care and protection is not followed, as described earlier. It is essential to have an open discussion with one's family physician about sexual practices and be evaluated with STD tests.

MAURICE IN A PANIC

It was only a small accident off the Saint-Laurent Boulevard in Montréal, and calling the police or ambulance didn't seem necessary on that Sunday morning. It was still a shocking experience for Maurice, a man in his mid-thirties, going to work as a barista in Vieux-Montréal, the old city.

He had stopped his car at a heavy pedestrian crosswalk and was daydreaming about his girlfriend, who was still studying in Caen, France, when a taxi van making a right-hand turn slid into his front left
fender.

Maurice was shocked to see the taxi's heavy grille in his face. Immediately, he felt panicked by the unexpected lurch and the noise of grinding metal.

Once Maurice's heart stopped thumping, he tried to catch his breath. He got out of his car to survey the damage and spoke to a passerby, who was about to call the police. "No, no police. No one's injured. There's no need," he shouted, trying to catch his breath.

After exchanging phone numbers and insurance information

LAWRENCE E. MATRICK M.D.

with the taxi driver, who was very polite and apologetic, Maurice drove away, physically unharmed but extremely on edge.

But three days later, when his boss asked him to drive across town and over a bridge to the Marriott hotel to make a special delivery, he felt the panic well up again.

When he got into his car with the package, he broke into a sweat. His hands were so wet and clammy that he couldn't grip the steering wheel. His heart was racing, he was gasping for breath, and his stomach was in his throat as he neared the bridge through heavy traffic.

He was able to drive to the hotel, just across the bridge, and got the door open just in time to vomit his breakfast onto the parking lot behind the Marriott where his delivery was. He waited, calmed down, and cleaned his face of bodily fluids. He then paid the door valet attendant to deliver the package.

He sat in his car and decided to immediately call his girlfriend, Daniela in France. *She'll be finished her history lectures at the college and be home now that its evening there*, he thought to himself. He gave a sigh of relief when she answered the phone.

He talked rapidly about his panic attacks. She could hear him gasping, but was very understanding. She encouraged him to seek help and move back with his mother, who was a nurse. "She'll take care of you, Maurice. She'll know what to do."

The next evening, he Skyped his girlfriend, Daniela, often crying into the laptop. He felt bewildered by his panic.

Again, she was very sympathetic and reassuring, but insisted he seek help. "You must see a doctor, *mon chéri*. It must be your heart. Remember? Your papa died of a bad heart attack," she shouted, wagging her finger at him.

What she said about his father dying threw him into an acute anxiety. Now, he was too frightened to see a doctor, lest he was told that his heart was damaged or that he was crazy.

At the same time, he also remembered that he and his friends at work had often made fun of a young woman who was very nervous and had a facial tic. Now that he was suffering from such periodic anxiety and his own facial tic with frequent blinking, he was sorry and felt guilty for laughing at her nervousness.

For months after, Maurice suffered from periodic severe headaches and nausea. He avoided driving and refused to drive to unfamiliar places or anywhere outside his immediate community. His boss had to find someone else to make those deliveries.

Maurice even felt nervous if he was a passenger in his friends' cars. He would hold on tight to the door handle and feel dizzy. He was always asking friends who were driving to "Take it easy," or "Please, slow down." They were getting tired of driving him, and him telling them what to do or how to drive.

After a while, he just stopped seeing his friends. He drank beer, smoked marijuana all day, and stayed home to play video games on his computer. He refused to answer Daniela's phone calls and moved in with his mother, as Daniela had suggested, where he felt safe.

After several weeks of this, Maurice's mother became more worried. She also suggested he see his family doctor.

"Are you kidding, Ma?" Maurice replied, lighting up another toke and downing his third beer of the morning, trying to relax. "He'll think I'm crazy. No way." He gulped for air and felt his pulse rate in his wrist.

"That small accident that you told me about was enough to set off these terrifying panic attacks. Especially whenever you drove your car, my boy. I read all about this at the library," she said sympathetically, taking his beer glass away from him.

A few days later, it was the chest pain again. The memory of his father in hospital with a heart attack forced him to be taken unwillingly to the emergency ward by Daniela. She was so worried about Maurice that she had come back from studying in France. It was she who dragged him to the hospital.

He was examined by the psych nurse and referred to Dr. Nazir, the on-call hospital psychiatrist. He told Maurice that he could be treated very quickly with mild medication plus psychotherapy, and that he had an excellent prognosis.

Maurice reluctantly agreed to outpatient therapy on the insistence of Daniela, who scolded him. "And you have to see Doctor Nazir for individual therapy. Or else." Maurice agreed because of the "or else," although she didn't elaborate at the time what she would do. Maurice thought to himself that she made that threat because their intimate relationship had disappeared due to his inability to have sex.

He therefore accepted a prescription for a fast-acting medication that he put under his tongue to dissolve. It gave him quick relief of his panic disorder.

During his third therapy session with the psychiatrist he pleaded. "I need this to be in the strictest of confidence, Doctor. My workplace is never to know, or the boys will always poke fun of me," he said sheepishly, taking his pulse rate again.

"And my boss will fire me if he finds out that I'm seeing a shrink," he added as he walked out.

Unfortunately, Maurice continued to drink heavily, which was counterproductive to taking his medication. It was also detrimental to his therapy sessions, since he often forgot about his appointments.

Daniela came to visit Maurice often. She was concerned about his mother's plight and her son's dependency on her and, now, on Daniela.

Daniela closed his bedroom door late one morning and sat beside him on his bed, where he was still in his pajamas. She was beside herself. She was being very supportive of her boyfriend, and yet he did very little to help himself. She decided to be strict and acted angrily to make him sit up and listen.

She belittled him and put on her best dramatic act. "You're too weak as a man, Maurice. Pull yourself together and smarten up. I need someone I can depend on, not a sniveling, complaining, grumpy wastrel. I'm outta here."

She left Maurice, and he never saw her again.

When she returned to her studies in Europe, she talked to her good friend, Celeste, when they met for tea at a local bar after their European history lecture. "I hope I did the right thing, *mon amie*. What would you have done?"

PANIC DISORDERS

A panic attack is an abrupt surge of intense fear or physical discomfort that reaches a peak within minutes. This abrupt surge can occur during a calm state with a terrifying accident, or when recalling a past history of some anxiety, as Maurice had with his father's cardiac condition.

The person will immediately suffer from a variety of symptoms, including cardiac complaints like palpitations, pounding heart, and chest pain, but also sweating, trembling, choking, dizziness, and a fear of dying. There may be breathing problems and stomach complaints like nausea, vomiting, or diarrhea. An overwhelming fear of unreality, feeling detached from others, and a sense of "going crazy" are not uncommon.

Maurice's panic disorder would have improved if he had taken his mother's advice about seeking treatment. She was severely affected by her son's despair, as was his girlfriend, Daniela.

His attitude had a distrustful and alarming effect on Daniela, such that she had to leave him.

Furthermore, his employment was affected, as were his friends. Had he been more forthright with his boss, he could have been on sick leave and his job preserved. His outcome would have improved if he had not kept it so confidential and had remained in therapy with his psychiatrist.

Such an attack as Maurice had most commonly follows a spell of stress or anxiousness about some event or interpersonal situation, like the threatened loss of a loved one or an impending health concern. Having one panic attack produces a sense of unease, and may trigger multiple future attacks.

It is not the result of some medical condition like drug abuse, other cardiopulmonary issues, or hyperthyroidism, which in themselves may have panic symptoms. It is also not better explained by post-traumatic stress disorder or some other, ongoing mental condition like social anxiety disorder or obsessive-compulsive disorder.

A panic disorder specifically refers to unexpected, ongoing, and recurrent attacks. It often occurs spontaneously, "out of the blue," or when resting or sleeping. It may occur without a visible precipitating event or cue.

An expected attack is usually triggered by some inner or external signal, like entering another stressful situation that originally triggered a minor attack in the distant past. The frequency of a panic disorder varies widely, and may be daily, weekly, or intermittent on a monthly basis. Persons who have more frequent attacks most likely have prolonged periods of stress, anxiety, or other mental problems. Medical problems will encourage more frequent attacks.

One type of unexpected panic attack is nocturnal—that is,

waking up from sleep in a state of severe discomfort and panic. Anxiety symptoms include breathing and cardiac complaints causing a fear of dying. A dream or nightmare about some daily, difficult, unfinished task or some daytime threat to one's medical health, interpersonal relationships, or workplace will trigger such a nocturnal episode.

Another common trigger is medication side effects occurring during sleep, or the addiction to drugs or alcohol.

Some cultures report a lesser incidence of this disorder with a lower prevalence. There appears to be a higher prevalence in the "white" population and generally among females. The disorder peaks during adolescence and early adulthood, and may decline in older individuals.

The course of such a disorder, if untreated, can become chronic, with episodic outbreaks for many years. However, it is often dependent on other ongoing mental or medical illnesses.

Risk factors and establishing a prognosis—that is, the future of the illness—is dependent on similar factors to phobias and other mental ills described earlier. Such risk factors include one's personal sensitivity outlook on life, introversion, a general sense of anxiety, and other, more familiar, mental and ongoing medical illnesses already explained under phobias. There may be a higher genetic risk if parents are predisposed to the disorder.

Once again, treatment is readily available. An evaluation by one's family physician is essential to rule out ongoing medical illnesses like diabetes, thyroid disorders, drug and alcohol addictions, or cardiovascular conditions. That physician would have a discussion as to other stress factors like relationship problems, employment difficulties, or other precipitating stressors. Medication prescribed by your physician will be most helpful.

Your physician may refer you to a psychiatrist for more intensive and less problematic medication or for psychotherapy. Psychologists will also provide excellent therapy, either individually or through group therapy.

As with other mental illnesses already discussed, activity, both social and physical, is rewarding. Talking about your situation with others and not hiding the illness is essential toward recovery.

ISABELLA AND WARTS

Isabella combed her beautifully-streaked, blonde hair in the mirror that the nurse had provided. She admired herself and smiled to see that she still looked pretty good for a fifty-year-old hooker.

I've still got another ten good years, she thought to herself. She felt assured that the European men still preferred an attractive, mature, dark-skinned woman with firm breasts and good legs—despite the itch down below in her groin.

"Especially after an expensive dinner, a good Cabernet, and a five-star hotel. Unlike these cheap Yanks and their 'wham-bam, thank you ma'am' types." She laughed to herself as she gave the mirror back to the nurse.

Isabella's musings were interrupted by the nurse, who looked up and asked her patient what she was talking about.

She didn't wait for the answer. "The doctor won't be too long, miss," the nurse said, covering her patient's pelvic area with the blue hospital gown. "You told the front desk that it was an emergency?" she asked, but quickly left the clinic room before Isabella answered.

Isabella's heart was racing; she was nervous to have her pelvis so intimately exposed in a foreign country. She was never this anxious to show herself so openly throughout Europe, since that was what she received the large number of euros for.

Today, she had to wait with her legs up in the stirrups in the gynecologist's examining room at the general hospital in Montréal. It was very embarrassing, but she was pleased to have found the private clinic attached to the hospital.

Having left Spain, she had chosen Montréal to live and work so that she could be closer to her daughter, who had an excellent job with Microsoft in the city. She felt comfortable with the French language, but nervous to be at the English-speaking private clinic. It was attached to the general hospital where she was willing to pay to get her rash treated.

Her English was quite good, since she traveled throughout Europe and was fluent in many languages as a professional prostitute. It was a respectable job in Spain, and much safer since she only serviced the wealthiest men in the best hotels in Barcelona.

She was eighteen when she paid for a fishing boat to drop her and forty others onto the Spanish shores at four in the morning. For other services rendered, the boat's captain settled her in a district where many Africans lived, having escaped the cruel dictatorship of Idi Amin in Uganda where she was born.

It was safety that she needed following her escape in her late teens from her abusive husband, who was later killed during the revolution.

She explained to the nurse who returned, "*Si, si,* sorry … yes. The long flight on Iberian Air out of Madrid to Montréal, even in first class, was excruciating with the redness and the uncontrollable itching. Down there. You know," Isabella said. She pointed her highly manicured fingers toward her rectum as the nurse, a young woman named Antoinette according to her badge, hurriedly prepared a tray for the doctor.

"Yes, it would be, I'm sure, Isabella. Terrible to have, I see. Ah, here he is now. Doctor Ivanovic," Antoinette said as the door opened to the private examining room.

The doctor was a middle-aged man with glasses, sparse, gray hair, a large paunch hanging over his belt, and an expensive suit and tie under his white coat.

"Hello," he said with a heavy Hungarian accent, looking at the hospital chart that the nurse handed him. "Miss La Guardia. Isabella? Can I call you Isabella?" he asked, rolling the chair and sitting down. He pulled the gown away and moved in front of Isabella's naked pelvis.

"Yes, that's perfectly all right, Doctor," she answered politely. Isabella immediately reached down and tried to scratch at the warts surrounding her pelvic area.

Dr. Ivanovic abruptly withdrew her hand and reprimanded her. "No, no, Isabella. Don't scratch. The nurse will give you a salve right now to calm the redness," he said, motioning to his nurse to apply the ointment sitting on the tray close by.

Antoinette pulled on the sterile latex gloves and immediately spread a white, creamy substance all over Isabella's genital and anal warts. "We also have the prescription pad ready for you, Doctor," the nurse added, sympathetically patting Isabella's hip.

"Yes. It's genital warts. Condylomata acuminata, we call it, Isabella. You should remember that diagnosis when you see your own physician next week," the doctor said, pulling off his own gloves and pushing them into the slot of the waste container, soon to be incinerated. "I will write those words down for you, Isabella," he added.

LAWRENCE E. MATRICK M.D.

"*Si,* I have heard those words from my friends in the business. A doctor in Madrid gave to me a herbal pill for them, but it was of little usefulness, Doctor. Can I continue to meet with you? I can pay privately," she asked hopefully.

The doctor nodded in agreement and gave Isabella a month's prescription for the ointment and some medication to calm the itch. "I'll see you again soon; this week, once you are more comfortable with the salve and the pills. Follow the directions closely; have your partner always use a condom, or he will become infected. I'll surgically remove those warts the best I can. It will take some time, but you will be much, much better," the doctor said.

He gave her an appointment for the next few days. He came to the head of the table, smiled, and gave Isabella his card with the appointment.

The nurse gently helped Isabella out of the stirrups and brought her skirt, very expensive, red, lacy underwear, and Gucci boots to put on. "A professional, you said, when I asked for your occupation, Miss La Guardia. A doctor or a lawyer? You changed your name?"

Isabella donned her clothes and sat to lace up her fine, leather boots, which she had bought in Paris. "Yes, my name was too difficult; but no, a professional prostitute. I worked throughout Europe," she explained without reservation and quite proudly.

Antoinette gave a loud gasp. After a moment she stifled her surprise, but was still intrigued by the wealth surrounding Isabella. There was a fine, expensive suit from Coco-Chanel, a Hermes cosmetic's bag from Barcelona, silk scarves, and fancy red underwear spread out before her.

She sterilized the stirrups and prepared the tray for the next patient. "I recall reading about such women in the French history books. Sex for money," she said. But now titillated with the idea, she sheepishly added, "Can I ask how often you work and what you would charge?"

"Yes, of course. Women are often interested and do ask. Like everything else, it depends on the economy, but if it is good then I do very well—and tax free," Isabella said, laughing. She finished dressing and dabbed herself with a scented red lipstick. "Unfortunately the economy tanked some years ago, as Spain was in trouble. I had to work selling perfume at Chanel for five years." She added, "That was a bummer."

The nurse handed Isabella her fancy, Louis Vuitton purse she knew to be worth a few thousand dollars. "My goodness, Miss LaGuardia. I couldn't have that much sex. They might abuse you or not pay."

Isabella laughed at the innocence and naïvety of some women as she sprayed herself with Chanel perfume. "Payment is always up front, my dear, and I put the money in the hotel receptionist's desk safe. The men at the desk all knew me, and I gave them a very handsome tip for their service. Usually the customers are older men, and just want someone who will lie with them, be quiet, and just listen to them, unlike their wives. Often not even getting an erection."

"Oh, my. You just listen and play with them? Do they mind you being a black woman?"

Isabella finished dressing and put on her designer Lanvin jacket. "No, not at all. Some preferred a darker, well-tanned woman; it was more titillating and mysterious."

Antoinette blushed and turned to hide her face. "Oh, my. Fun and mysterious? I couldn't," she said, but was still curious.

"Ah ha, but playing in a *ménage à trois* is the most fun, and double the income for me, my dear." She hesitated and in anger, exclaimed, "And now I fear that it was the politician's wife who had the warts. *Merde*! I should have charged them triple. It was she who infected me. I saw them on her thighs." Isabella slammed her fist onto the table next to her.

"*Ménage à trois?* You mean a family of three?"

"*Oui*. And as an Antoinette, your name, you could add 'Marie,' who said, 'Let them eat cake.' It was a widespread practice when the real Marie Antoinette lived with that king, Louis the sixteenth, in France, before he was guillotined. A three-way was not uncommon then. Some men preferred two women, explaining that they got two for one, but any combination was acceptable," she added with a toothy smile.

"Maybe then. But not since, Miss LaGuardia," the nurse retorted as she cleaned the stirrups and threw the covers and sheets in the laundry basket. Still titillated by the exposure to so much sexual knowledge, she waited.

"Well, perhaps you didn't know that the admiral atop of Trafalgar square in London, Lord Horatio Nelson, was in a three-way with a Lady, Emma Hamilton, and her husband. Well … until he was killed five years later in that naval battle. As was the famous psychoanalyst, Carl Jung, who had his wife sleep with one of his teenaged patients as a three-way for many years."

The nurse blushed and put her hands up to her face in shock. She wanted to ask more, but was afraid of being too nosey, being rebuked, or getting too much information that she couldn't handle.

Instead, she shook her head in earnest and began her usual nurse's lecture. "Get your customers to use condoms so you won't infect the men, Miss LaGuardia, or their wives or other girlfriends, with genital warts," she said and added, "As the good doctor said, you must insist on condoms from here on in." She was ready to leave.

Just as the nurse walked away, she stopped and asked, "With all those rich men, did you fall in love and marry?" She waited patiently as Isabella put on more lipstick and brought out an expensive eye makeup casing from her Hermes bag.

"Yes. In love many times. It drove me crazy, however; I was married to three. Drove me insane, nurse. Crazy, indeed, and I was nervous, anxious, panic-struck."

"My, my. How terrible for you. What did you do?"

Isabella grinned. "Nothing. I decided that whoever said, 'Love is a temporary insanity, curable only by marriage', was right," she said, laughing.

Antoinette nodded and laughed in unison. But just before the nurse reached the door, Isabella hurriedly called her back. "Nurse! Will the good doctor come back soon and explain what that accumulation of warts means? What they will do to me? Will I be well again? I need to work, Nurse, and this must be kept confidential."

"Yes, yes, very confidential. The doctor will be right back to explain the surgical procedure. The word is condylomata acuminata. It is an accumulation of warts. He will tell you all about it. And you will be well enough to get back to that work of yours. And with the condoms for your customers. Buy some," she said in a huff, prepared to leave Isabella to wait for the doctor.

"Wait. Please wait. I'm afraid, nurse. Is all this private? You know, in confidence. My livelihood, my work, depends on it."

Antoinette stopped. "Yes, yes. This is all very confidential, as I said, but you need to see a psychiatrist for your anxiety and learn how to get a real job."

Isabella tossed that remark off as she finished dressing. She lovingly fingered the doctor's card and put it in her purse. "He assured me that he can remove those warts. I'm too old to keep doing this, getting infections. Maybe I'll get a good job with Chanel, here in Montréal, and move closer to be with my daughter," she muttered to herself and waited for the doctor to return.

GENITAL WARTS

G enital warts are a sexually transmitted disease (STD): the result of specific types of human papillomavirus (HPV), types 6 and 11. This disease has been known since before Christ and described by Hippocrates, a famous physician in 300 BCE.

The warts are easy to recognize by being on the surface of the skin, pink in color, often itchy, and at times painful. They appear several months after skin-to-skin exposure and following genital, oral, or anal sex.

A condyloma acuminatum is a single genital wart. Condylomata acuminata are multiple genital warts. These words are derived from Greek, meaning "a pointed wart."

Diagnosis is generally obvious, and a biopsy will confirm the likelihood. They may develop in clusters or by themselves, and are usually in the pelvic area, around the female genitals and outer labia, on the male penis and scrotum, or close to the anus. The internal organs like the cervix, vagina, the urethral opening, or in the rectum are not immune to the virus.

This disease has, like all the other STDs, become prevalent once again partly due to ignorance and greatly due to transmission as outlined in Isabella's work history.

Multiple partners who carry the virus produce multiple rampant infections, which are then distressing for the individual. They can cause severe anxiety and depression. The medical system is overwhelmed, and the economic cost is huge for the individual with loss of work and the potential loss of relationships.

Transmission of warts is usually through skin-to-skin contact and often by sexual, anal, or oral sex. Condoms can be protective for the male, but may not be helpful in prevention for females. The possibility of infection is very high if one partner demonstrates warts.

Treatment can be very effective, but recurrence can be spontaneous after a latent period, and symptoms can reappear after some time.

The warts may be the only symptom of disease. Itchiness, redness, occasional pain, or bleeding may occur. Masses of warts may appear, and they may be quite hard to the touch, with a small stalk like that of a mushroom. Some people may be overcome with anxiety or depression following the outbreak.

Warts can be transmitted to the newborn during birth with passage through the birth canal. If the parent touches their own warts, then the children can be infected through parental touching while changing diapers, through that skin-to-skin contact.

Prevention is by the use of condoms and by some HPV vaccines. Treatment is with specific creams prescribed by your physician, cryotherapy, or surgical excision. Some warts may disappear after some time without active treatment.

Treatment generally is by physical removal (that is, by ablation) or by the use of topical agents and creams. Cryosurgery, or the use of liquid nitrogen, can be performed in the office by a physician.

Some may use laser ablation, but larger clusters may require an anesthetic and surgical excision. Scarring from such therapy may occur and be problematic, depending on the site.

If left untreated, the virus can cause cervical, vulvar, vaginal, or penile and rectal cancers. Similarly, oral cancers can occur in both sexes.

There is a high incidence of warts in the sexually active if care is not followed, such as through preventative techniques or by vaccines in the adolescent population. The incidence of infection is now in the upper millions in the USA and Canada, and cancers from HPV are extremely high.

Vaccines are now available for young teenaged boys and girls. It has been reported that young girls who are vaccinated are less likely to have sexual intercourse at a much earlier age, and they are more aware of prevention due to education. They are also less likely to use alcohol or drugs, or to become pregnant, according to many experts.

The best prevention is to be in a monogamous relationship, or to have sex with one who is free of the disease. If there is any doubt, then an evaluation by a physician is mandatory. A routine screening for women can prevent cervical cancer. However, some doctors may not test for HPV or other sexually transmitted diseases routinely during an office visit.

Some other STDs one should be tested for, if in doubt, are chlamydia, genital herpes, syphilis, gonorrhea, and also hepatitis B. Pregnant women who may be vulnerable to STDs due to their history should likewise be tested for those STDs but also for HIV (the cause of AIDS), which has been recurring again.

CHARLIE:
A PROBLEMATIC PERSONALITY

It was four o'clock on Thursday afternoon. Dr. Jason McNeill was just closing his office door and ready to go home. That day, he had seen seven patients in his private psychiatric office in downtown Calgary, and he was tired. Before leaving, he checked Friday's schedule with his receptionist, Maria.

"Busy day, tomorrow, Doctor McNeill: a full house. Hope there's no emergencies before the weekend," she said, showing him the list and drumming her fingers on the open appointment book.

It was just then that the phone rang. Maria answered it and called out to the doctor just as he reached the outer door. "It's Mr. John Ortis, the lawyer. Says it's urgent to speak with you, Doctor."

McNeill groaned but waited at the door, wondering if he should just walk out.

"Shall I tell him you've gone, Doctor?" Maria said, covering the phone speaker with her hands to keep it private.

The psychiatrist hesitated. Ortis referred many of his clients to him for independent medical examinations. It was after car accidents and for a psychiatric opinion.

This must be another one of those, he thought to himself. He never called personally and always had his legal secretary make the referral. "Okay, I'll take it. Must just want a quick opinion, Maria. Thanks," McNeill said, walking back and picking up Maria's phone.

"Hi, Doctor. Thanks for taking my call. He said he'd kill himself, doc. If he goes back into jail. You remember Charlie? He's terrified. Phobic, I guess, of spiders."

"Arachnophobia, John. Nice Irishman. Wouldn't see me again after he punched his girlfriend out, and I told him I couldn't help him. Said he was too busy, anyway. The guy's a born liar. Needs abuse therapy at the clinic."

"Yes, too busy breaking into houses also. Second-story thief. You said he was a sociopath. He wouldn't see you again two years ago, but now he's said he'll kill himself if the judge throws him in jail again. Said he can't stand tight enclosures now."

"Claustrophobic, John. Claustrophobic."

"Yep. Now specializes in wealthy, underground car parking garages. Lexus, Audis. High-priced cars. Too fearful of high places, now. Can't go up two stories, doc."

"Acrophobic, John. Phobic of heights. Charlie's in big trouble with all those phobias, sure, but still a personality disorder. I'll see him tomorrow one more time. I'll call you."

"Thanks. Careful with him; he has a short fuse. Gets belligerent if you cross him. Bugger lifted my beautiful digital clock off my desk when I turned my back. Said he'd pay me back. Liar and a damn crook, but still suicidal, doc."

Dr. Jason McNeill hung up the phone and looked at the Friday schedule for the next day in his appointment book. "Maria, call Ortis and get Charlie O'Flanagan in at 10:45 tomorrow morning.

Call Sara Johnson and tell her to come in at 11:15 instead of 11 AM. We'll squeeze Charlie in. Watch your purse. Oh, also, the cops may bring him."

Indeed, at 10:30 the next morning Charlie O'Flanagan was escorted into the psychiatrist's office by a big, burly, tattooed police officer and a young rookie female who kept trying to avoid Charlie's wandering paws.

Fifteen minutes later, Dr. McNeill opened his consultation room door and said good-bye to his patient. He looked at Charlie and told him to come in.

The trio stood, and the officers started to walk in with Charlie, who looked tense and worried.

"It's okay, officers; I'll be okay with Charlie here. Just wait in the outer room. We'll be about half an hour," McNeill said, shaking Charlie's hand and ushering him in.

Maria looked at the doctor, who nodded at her purse. She winked and put her purse in the desk drawer and locked it.

McNeill sat in his chair next to one side of his large, floor-to-ceiling window overlooking the Bow River and the city of Calgary from the fifteenth floor. "Have a chair, Charlie," the doctor said, motioning to his patient to sit in the opposite chair near the window.

Charlie had stopped at the door and looked around. He then took the large, heavy chair and dragged it close to the door, away from the window.

Charlie pointed to the scene outside. "The Bow River. Like, called so by the aboriginals. Made their bows from the reeds. You know along the river. Did so," he explained, pointing out the window.

"I didn't know that, Charlie. Okay, Mr. O'Flanagan. Tell me, what's been going on since we last met some time ago? By the way, did you bring my secretary's silver pen set back? You know,

the one you lifted when you were here the last time." The doctor
waited patiently.

Charlie shifted in his chair. He was in his early sixties, balding
with a small, gray beard and mustache. He was very wiry and of
small stature, but still quite muscular and strong.

"Naw. Not me, doc. Like, I don't need that crap. Look, the judge
said he would put me back. In prison. I'm already on probation. You
know, to be with my friends, he said. Caught stealing the wheels off
a Lexus. Like, with my friend. Stupid bastard. Set off the alarm."

McNeill was amazed at how he spoke in short, quick sentences.
He took his time as he looked about the office, but refused eye
contact and kept checking out the desk and the nice paintings on
the walls.

"I thought you were a second-story man, Charlie."

Charlie waited. "Got a cigarette, doc? Don't smoke? Like, bad
for you. And I was. Got height sick, once. Prefer the rich condos.
You know apartments. Much easier; only the underground parking.
Easy peasy. Gonna lock me up? Like, in the loony bin? I'm always
sad, now. Can't sleep. Nervous, like a scared rabbit. You know, shit,
crying."

McNeill thought quickly about how to help this man. A sociopath,
but depressed and suffering from phobias. "I'll put you on an anti-
depressant that will also help your anxiety and phobias. If you agree
to see me weekly and take the meds, then I'll write a medical-legal
report for the judge, through your lawyer. I think that will keep you
out of prison. Much cheaper for the government, Charlie."

Charlie finally grinned. He got up and gazed out the window,
but never got close to it. "Do it. I'll do it. Like, I can pay you.
Whatever it takes. Judge O'Toole. Nice guy. You know, he'll go
for it," he said, smirking. He walked into the corner of the room

and riffled through a medical journal on the desk.

McNeill thought, *Maybe I've been taken in by this thief. Snookered. I'll take a chance.* He wrote out a prescription from his chair near the window. He handed it to Charlie. "Take one tablet twice a day, Charlie. See your parole officer regularly. Take a holiday from stealing, or your friend the judge will throw the key away. Deal?"

Charlie wiped the sweat from his brow as the doctor turned to get his chair back in place near the window. "Deal, doc. It's a deal. Like, next week? What time? Thanks, doc." He turned to the door, sweating, and left without a "good bye" or "how do you do."

McNeill finished making his notes and quickly dictated a medical legal report in his office for Ortis. He took it out to his secretary to edit and then told her to send it to the lawyer once he signed it.

McNeill walked back into his office but came out again, swearing. "Damn it, Maria. He fingered the new gold pen on my desk that my daughter gave me for my birthday when I turned my back on him."

"I warned you, Doctor. Nimble fingers."

Charlie indeed keep all his appointments with his parole officer. It was after the judge accepted McNeill's report and put him on a two-year suspended sentence, with certain provisions that he must keep. He was always on time to see the psychiatrist, took his meds faithfully, and started a "Keep Fit" program at the local YMCA.

His depression, anxiety, and phobias were responding to the meds, and he kept out of trouble for a whole four weeks. But he denied ever taking that gold pen. "Like, you musta lost it, doc. You know, somewhere."

It was on the fifth week of therapy that he confessed to the doctor. "Sorry, doc, but I couldn't resist. Here's your pen back. Nice.

Back at it, you know. Poorly locked garage. Like, adjoining that massive house. On Glendale Ave," he said, sitting in the psychiatrist's desk chair far away from the windows.

McNeill counted the three paintings on his walls and moved his desk's digital clock closer to his side where he sat in the large chair by the windows.

McNeill swiveled his chair away from the window to face Charlie. "That was dumb, Charlie. If the police catch you, then I won't be able to help you and no one else will, man," he said, taking the pen from Charlie. He put it in his suit jacket pocket.

Charlie lowered his head, scratched his sparse beard, and waited to be chastised again. Almost like a child in front of his mother. "Tried to, doc. Like, you know, to hold back, doc. Couldn't. Shoulda. Didn't. But nice lady, that Clarice," he said with a sheepish smile.

"Clarice?"

"Yeah, doc. She caught me. You know, rifling her new Lexus. Like, in her underground. You know."

The doctor was exasperated with such foolishness. But now he was the fool for trying to help a sociopathic personality. But he still had to see this through. "No, I didn't know, Charlie. Tell me."

At this point, Charlie went into a long story about his inability to pass on a quick, "easy-peasy job," as he proudly said again. As he talked, he walked about, but never close to the windows. He spoke in soft tones, often in a hush, but always in short, staccato sentences.

He explained that he had cased out Springfield Street in the wealthy area of Calgary last year, and had done some second-story work there. He had to stop due to his fear of heights, but always remembered #36 in Glendale with spacious grounds and the garage adjoining the opulent manor.

On that day the garage was closed, but he had no trouble using one of the many remote door openers that he had stolen from other undergrounds.

"You take all those remotes?"

"Naw. Like, I'm not stupid, doc. I only take one remote. Managers never change them all. So that one, you know: it's still working. Often opens up other garages. Did this one. Like, just passing by, I was," he explained with a smart-aleck laugh.

"Just passing by, where you? Should have stayed home in bed, Charlie."

Charlie nodded sheepishly, but explained about Clarice. The problem occurred when he was walking between the Lexus and the Saab, checking the doors and finding the windows to both cars half open.

"The lady who caught me. Said she always leaves the windows down. So crooks don't have to break. You know: the windows and doors. Saves her money, you know, and hassle with insurance."

"Yes, I know. Sounds like a good idea, Charlie. Always a problem with getting the car fixed, and a hassle with the insurance," the psychiatrist said. He watched Charlie pick his teeth with a match stick.

Charlie's story continued to unravel. Slowly. "Nice lady, Clarice. Scared the bee-Jesus outta me, doc. Like, said she was just looking for her cat. I had some money. From the Saab, her car. You know: some high-tech stuff. Flashlights. Radio. Keys. Scarves. All from the Lexus. Also hers. Oh, and a cell. You know: a nice camera."

"You did well. Just passing by, were you?"

"Yeah. She says to me. She says. Look, give me my camera, my cell, and scarves. I'll give you cash; will save you selling that stuff. She says to me, you know." He stopped to spit the match stick, broken in half, onto the floor.

"So what happened? She called the police."

"Naw. Invited me in for a cup of tea. Said she couldn't sleep. Asked me if I like to garden. I do. Hubby died last year. After tea, at five in the morning, I need to go for a leak. You know, bladder trouble. And she asks me if I would move in. Like, downstairs, in her basement suite. Do the garden. Other repairs in the house. House, you know, needs fixing up. Like, I told her I can do."

McNeill thought that a woman could calm Charlie down and keep him on the straight and narrow.

He continued to see Charlie throughout that year. He had a story each time, and was pleased to confess to the psychiatrist. To unburden himself of a lifetime of thievery, debauchery, periodic drug addictions, alcoholic bouts with fist fights, aggressive sexual assaults on women he'd lived with, hospitalizations after bar brawls, alley fights, and three suicide attempts.

It was one of the last times that he came to see the psychiatrist that Charlie told him about Clarice again. After only one month of living in the basement suite, she'd invited him up to her bedroom. Charlie got prescriptions for Viagra from his doctor, and she took him with her on long, extended holidays.

"Like, mostly Holland America cruising, doc. She's a horny lady, doc. You know, menopausal, so not going to get pregnant. Like, nice," he said, asking for another prescription of anti-depressants as he left.

McNeill never saw him after that. He just never showed up again.

Two years later, Ortis phoned and told him that Charlie was back in jail. "He was caught stealing in an underground parkade. He attempted suicide twice while serving his two years. Clarice visited him in the prison hospital a few times while he was recovering from the overdose."

"She did?"

"Yes. She wanted to know what pawn shop he had hocked her jewelry at, which he had stolen from her while she was asleep. So she could try and get her necklace and rings back, you know priceless family heirlooms. She told him he was a cheat: a no-good bum, and it was too bad that he hadn't succeeded in killing himself, since they'd had such a good life together."

"Sorry to hear that. What else did she say?"

"Told him he wasn't worth his salt."

The doctor scratched his head. "Where did that come from, not worth your salt?"

"Yeah. Salt was a necessary commodity, and the Roman army was paid in bags of salt, or what they called a '*salarium.*' Thus our word, 'salary.' If they were poor soldiers, then they weren't 'worth their salt,' like she said to Charlie, and didn't get their *salarium.* Our word 'salary' was thus coined, Doctor."

"Right. 'Salt of the earth' and 'a grain of salt' are other sayings. Bright lady, Clarice. Did she leave after that?"

Ortis thought for a moment. "Oh, not quite. Told him that he mustn't ever tell anyone they knew each other. She was too embarrassed to know him and to sleep with a thief. Wanted it all to be 'hush-hush.' Never got her jewelry back," Ortis said to McNeill before he hung up.

McNeill felt sorry for Charlie, and sorrier for Clarice. He said so to his receptionist after the phone call from Ortis.

"He was a nice guy, as all psychopathic personality disorders are, Doctor. He brought me a bouquet of flowers occasionally," Maria said as the doctor started to walk out for the day.

The doctor stopped and thought for a minute. "Yes, he was. I'll go and see him at the prison hospital. Make sure he's on the right anti-depressants and getting supportive therapy. Maybe get him an early parole if he promises to get back into therapy." McNeill opened the door to leave.

Maria reminded the doctor of his next day's appointments. "You know, he even sort of came on to me when he was last here, Doctor. I thought it was cute," she said with a smile.

McNeill turned back. "He did? Why didn't you tell me? Was he abusive to you?"

"Not really. Charlie just looked me up and down when I was at the file cabinet, patted my bum, and tried to feel me up."

McNeill was incensed. "So? What did you do?"

"I told him to keep his hands to himself. He only said that one thing more to me ... he said, 'if I told you that you had a beautiful body, would you hold that against me?'"

"Typical Charlie," McNeill said with a laugh and walked out.

PERSONALITY DISORDERS

A person with a personality disorder can be very difficult to diagnose because there is such a large category of these types of disorders. Charlie, in the above fiction story, is relatively straightforward because of his long history of thievery and disregard for other's feelings. He was only interested in his own welfare, despite jail time, therapy, and what his family or society thought of him. He would be classified as a sociopathic type of personality disorder.

Personality disorders are a class of mental disorders. They have totally disturbed, unusual, and maladaptive ways of behaving and thinking, and they have inner, ingrained experience that they then act out in society. Such behaviors and thought processes deviate widely from the norm and what could be acceptable in that person's culture.

The term "personality" is, by definition, a set of enduring, stable, and permanent behaviors and mental traits that distinguish individual humans. A person with a personality disorder has totally different experiences and behaviors, which differ from social norms and deviate from societies' expectations. They experience problems in cognition, thinking, emotions, interpersonal functioning, and impulse control.

Such individuals lack understanding, that is insight, into their thoughts and behaviors and could care less as to how their behaviors are perceived. They have serious problems in interpersonal relationships, in impulse control, and in social and occupational functioning. Such attitudes produce enormous costs to the community in police work and for the court system.

Any relationships that develop are fleeting, untrustworthy, disruptive, and short-lived. Charley demonstrated this even in the close, comfortable lifestyle that he briefly had with Clarice. Her jewelry was far too enticing for him.

As with Charley, such personalities can still suffer from anxiety and depression because of their legal and family complications, but they are essentially devoid of guilt or remorse for their actions.

The diagnosis can be problematic due to cultural norms and cultural expectations, and even as far as social, sociopolitical, and economic considerations are concerned. Thus thievery, corruption, or other pseudo-legal activities in some societies can be seen to be acceptable.

In general, personality disorders are diagnosed in almost one-half of psychiatric patients, and thus makes them the most frequent of all psychiatric diagnoses. These behavior patterns are typically seen in adolescence or early adulthood, but can be observed even in children.

Classification of such disorders becomes problematic due to cultural expectations or even sociopolitical and economic expectations. However, there is a consensus that several criteria are required to arrive at such a diagnosis.

There must be an enduring pattern that deviates from the usual expectations of one's culture. Such deviation must be in thinking, emotions, interpersonal functioning, and in impulse control. It must be inflexible and pervasive, and it must lead to distress or impairment in social, occupational, and all other areas of functioning.

It must be stable, of long duration, and traced back to early adulthood or teen years.

Finally, it is not part of another mental disorder, be due to addictions, or part of another medical condition like a head trauma.

Generally there are ten types: paranoid, schizoid, schizotypal, antisocial, borderline, histrionic, narcissistic, avoidant, dependent, and obsessive-compulsive. These are then grouped into three clusters. "Odd or eccentric" include the schizoid, schizotypal, and paranoid. "Dramatic and emotional" are the antisocial, borderline, histrionic, and narcissistic types. Finally, the "anxious or fearful" types are the avoidant, dependent, and obsessive-compulsive types.

Those who do suffer from such disorders may be totally devoid of insight—that is, understanding—and are thus very reluctant to seek or accept treatment. Some may be encouraged by family, friends, or society to seek treatment and may be willing to accept change because of the disruption, which they might finally accept to be unhealthy.

Narcissistic and the obsessive-compulsive types have a higher level of functioning, and can be more successful in life than all other types due to their ability to interact, be employed, and be pleasant to be with.

Addictions, other mental disorders affecting the individual, and head trauma can be very complicating to diagnose as to their overall functioning or to get them involved in treatment.

The paranoid type has a pervasive distrust and suspiciousness of all others, often beginning in childhood. They suspect that others are exploiting, harming, or deceiving them. Such a paranoid person is preoccupied with doubts and reluctant to confide in or trust others. They see hidden meanings in relationships and communications and think that others want to harm them. They are difficult to get along with, often accuse their friends or loved ones of cheating on them, and may be prepared to do harm to them.

The schizoid personality has a pattern of detachment from social relationships with a restricted range of emotions. They are solitary, avoid close relationships, and have little interest in sexual bonding. There is a sense of indifference, detachment, coldness, and avoidance of activities.

The schizotypal are very eccentric, and similarly avoid close interactions, have odd beliefs or magical thinking, odd thinking and speech, and could be very suspicious or even overtly paranoid at times.

Antisocial personalities are often deceitful, lie, are willing to con others, cheat, steal, and are impulsive, irritable, aggressive, reckless, totally irresponsible, and lack remorse or guilt for their violation of others. Often, the adolescent demonstrates a conduct disorder, which leads to problems in school and then in their employment. Charlie, in the above fiction story, was a good example.

A disturbance in identity, interpersonal relationship problems, poor self-image, impulsivity, fear of abandonment, reckless spending, substance abuse, binge eating, and recurrent suicidal behaviors are all paramount in the borderline type. They also have intense anger issues, get into fights and quarrels, and have a transient, wandering existence.

The histrionic constantly seeks drama, to act out, and be on stage; they need to be the center of attention. They are shallow characters when not acting out and are very suggestible.

Narcissus, the Greek god, saw his facial reflection in a pool of water and immediately fell in love with himself. The narcissistic needs admiration and adoration. They are preoccupied with themselves and their brilliance, exaggerate their accomplishments, and constantly seek power, beauty, and ideal love. They take advantage of others and are dismissive of others' needs or feelings. The majority are male.

Avoidant types of personalities show a pattern of isolation, a sense of inadequacy, and are hypersensitive. They avoid close contact for fear of rejection, and are fearful of criticism. They see themselves to be inadequate, unappealing to others, and are easily embarrassed.

The dependent personality constantly seeks reassurance and needs to be cared for with a clinging attitude. They are indecisive, anxious, and basically can't do things for themselves. They quickly seek out others to depend on if they lose their first love.

Obsessive-compulsive personalities are just that. They obsess about neat and tidiness and are preoccupied with thoughts of orderliness, perfectionism, and inner control at the expense of flexibility and openness. Unfortunately, they lose the total picture due to perfectionism in the small details. They are compulsive in rituals and are rigid, inflexible, and over-conscientious in work or play. Finally, they would rather do it themselves than delegate work to others.

Chronic medical conditions can lead to any of the above personality disorders. Traumatic brain injuries, chronic infections, substance abuse, or tumors in the body (plus more serious mental disorders) can cause personality disturbance.

The causes of personality disorders can be multiple. Childhood trauma like sexual and physical abuse, chronic verbal abuse, and overprotective parental attitudes may be causal factors. Heredity is a factor and needs further exploration.

Therapy is available, and a qualified psychologist can offer cognitive and family therapy on an office basis or at a rehabilitation center. A family physician who has some expertise and time can be most helpful. Such a physician can refer to a psychiatrist for further cognitive treatment and to prescribe medication to reduce the anxiety, depression, or any associated mental anguish.

Inpatient hospital treatment may be required or, unfortunately, a prison sentence, as in Charlie's situation. However, prisons have excellent councilors or visiting therapists.

MISTER CHEUNG'S ALZHEIMER'S

Lucille feared that there was something wrong with her father when he started to tell her that she had four brothers and two sisters still living in China. She later discovered from her mother that indeed he had a good memory for past events, but he could no longer recall his daughter's name.

Her mother was now seriously ill with pancreatic cancer, and her father was up all night, wandering about and disturbing the neighbors with his complaints of noise and dogs barking.

"Lucy," as her mother called her, began to visit her parents more often and was surprised to hear that she had siblings elsewhere, according to her father.

She vividly remembered him insisting on her managing the grocery store and the adjoining small café in their town in northern Ontario while he went to the bank or to buy groceries for the café. She was only fifteen then; the eldest, with a younger brother that she had to care for while her mother worked in the local paper mill.

It wasn't too long before her father would send her to the bank to get a money order made out to some woman called Huang.

He then had her post the money to this woman living in central Beijing. Lucille had never asked about that, since as a young, loyal, and obedient daughter, she never could in dutiful respect to her father.

Now that she was older and married with children, she explained some of this to her brother, who lived in the lower basement rooms in her own home across town. "He's getting strange, Ernest. He can't cope with Mamma's complaints of stomach problems and has struck out at her. She told me so, Ernie."

"Yeah, well, he came down to my room when he came to visit you and wanted something, but he forgot what he came for. I told him to go find his daughter, and she'll help you."

"What did he do?"

"Do? Nothing. He just stood there with a blank look on his face and scratched at his crotch. Said, 'Daughter? Do I have a daughter? They are in China. All of them.'" Then he opened my closet, and walked in."

"He needs help, Ernie. You need to get involved for once."

Ernie just shrugged his shoulders and went back to his accounting business. "I'm busy. It's February, and my clients need their tax forms ready for April, Lucy. You're the elder daughter. Go find him. Maybe take him and see a doctor."

After the neighbors complained about his knocking on their doors at nighttime and asking for "my number-one wife from China and all my children," she made the visits more often.

It was on such a visit that her mother showed Lucille the bruises on her back from her father pushing her. It was then that she decided to take her father that next week to see the doctor.

It was only the next day that the police called her to say that her father had called 911. "He was complaining that there was a strange lady in the kitchen, Mrs. Chen. When we got there, we only found your mother making dinner. He calmed down after talking for an hour with the social worker who came with us," the sergeant explained.

At the doctor's office that next week, the physician did a thorough examination. "He has some weakness on one side. Maybe a small stroke, or a brain tumor. I'll refer him to a neurologist, Lucille."

"Sorry for my father's appearance. It was the only way he would come to see the doctor," she explained to the receptionist when she escorted her father into the neurologist's office. She then added, "Our family doctor, Doctor Yu, thought that he might have a brain tumor." She gently maneuvered her father into a nearby chair.

The receptionist smiled and nodded as she typed in some details into the chart. She had heard this many times. "Thank you, Mrs. Chen. Doctor Parkinson will see your father shortly. Please have a seat."

As Lucille sat next to her father, she was visibly embarrassed. Her father was dressed in a blue toque, a glove on his left hand, and a ragged sweater over a pajama top. She tried not to look at her father's open-toed sandals with his dirty feet sticking out.

He had insisted on wearing his tennis shorts over his pajama bottoms. "I need to get my tennis racket, Lucille, before we go play," he explained to his daughter before he agreed to go with her.

It wasn't long before the doctor opened his consulting room. He walked over to his receptionist, reviewed the history she gave him, and asked Miss Chen to bring her father into his office.

Dr. Parkinson sat back in his chair behind his desk and looked at Mr. Cheung. He then opened his laptop and reviewed several hospital outpatient examinations.

Before the doctor could say anything, Lucille blurted out, "My father wouldn't leave his room, Doctor. I wasn't able to get him dressed. I'm sorry that he's dressed like this, but he eats, sleeps, and walks about dressed this way: in his tennis shorts. Loved the game, years ago."

"Does he exercise? Still play? Physical exercise would be healthy for his memory disorder."

"No. He stopped playing when his close friends who played tennis with him died. Now he still talks about visiting them. I've lost my father; our children lost their grandfather; my mother lost her husband. He doesn't care, and tries to joke about everything. It makes me so sad to have lost him, Doctor. He's like a robot now, a stranger."

The doctor had a sympathetic look as he closed his laptop. He smiled at Lucille's father, who smiled back as he pulled his pajama string on and off. "It's all right, Miss Chen. Your father had chest x-rays, blood work, and an MRI of his head, Miss Chen. Doctor Yu did a very thorough physical examination. He was concerned about your father's weakness on his left side and some changes to his frontal lobes on the MRI."

Lucille Chen shifted anxiously in her chair and wiped the mist out of her eyes with a tissue. Her father was oblivious to the remarks and kept trying to loosen a strap and remove a sandal. He almost fell over as he attempted this act.

Lucille caught him in time. "And his brain tumor? Can you cure his brain tumor?" she asked with an apprehensive look on her face.

"I don't see any evidence of a tumor, Miss Chen. Doctor Yu reports that your father has a long history of diabetes, cholesterol problems, and periodic, small strokes from a cardiovascular disorder. I'll do a thorough physical examination today. I suspect that he has what we now call Alzheimer's, Miss Chen. His MRI confirms that. We call it a chronic neurocognitive disorder."

"But … but, a tumor? Is it possible that he can be cured of a tumor?"

Parkinson shook his head as he scanned the MRI exam again. "No. The radiologist found no tumors, Miss Chen. But Doctor Yu did well to send your father to me for a further examination. We can offer him some medication that may delay any further progression of his dementia. But you can stay while I examine him. Let's just help him over to my examining table."

Lucille helped her father up and moved him to the table. He balked at the attempt and said something in Chinese, to which Lucille cringed.

"He went downhill after my mother became ill last year, Doctor. His memory is very poor now, and he refuses to sell the home and move in with my husband and me. He leaves the stove on. I'm afraid of a fire and any further abuse to my mother," she explained.

The doctor lifted Cheung's pajama top and listened to his chest. "Yes. This type of Alzheimer's is often precipitated by some trauma. A bereavement, any type of economic loss, a move out of the home, or an accident maybe."

"Yes, he stumbled down the basement stairs in his home and had a bad fall. He was very dependent on my mother before she became ill. Then their dog died," Lucille said as she watched the doctor do a complete physical and neurological examination.

"I suspect his deterioration began just before she fell ill, with all those changes and losses that he suffered. But I couldn't find any paralysis on his left side other than a general weakness," the doctor said to Lucille.

Mr. Cheung put his toque back on but stayed on the table.

"I should check his prostate just to be complete. Do you want to stay in the room?"

"I'll just turn around. Let me talk to him to keep him calm, Doctor," she answered as she turned toward the wall. She spoke kindly to her father in Chinese.

"You know, it was when he kept getting lost in the neighborhood that we worried more. Forgot the names of our friends and then his grandchildren. Finally, he called out that there was a strange woman in the house. My dear mother was in the kitchen fixing his dinner," she explained with much sorrow.

Once the doctor was finished with the rectal, he gave Mr. Cheung a tissue to clean himself. Cheung didn't know what to do with the tissue and handed it to Lucille. She gently cleaned his pelvic area. The doctor took it and threw it in the garbage tin.

"I know that your Chinese community has an excellent care home for such patents. I occasionally visit the 'Sung Yan Sun' care facility, and they would take good care of your father."

Lucille helped her father off the table and pulled up his pajama bottoms and helped him to dress. As she escorted him out of the room, she stopped briefly.

"Oh, dear. He has become so attached to Bingo, his good friend now. I hope they will accept Bingo also."

"Bingo?"

"Yes, Doctor. His little Bingo that he loves to play with. He takes it to bed now. It's a small mechanical dog. I worry because he takes it for a walk, and everyone laughs at him. When I watched him interacting with Bingo on his bed so lovingly last night, a tear came to my eye. I hadn't seen him smile like that for months."

"I know many with Alzheimer's who do well with pets. They are very comforting to my patients who have dementia."

Lucille took out a comb and brushed her father's wispy, gray hairs back off his face. "Why do you call it Alzheimer's?" she asked the doctor as she got her father ready to leave.

The doctor finished writing out the prescriptions. "Alzheimer's? Good question. Actually a neurologist, Alzheimer, in the last century noticed that some young people suffered from a pre-senile dementia in their early-to mid-forties. They died before they were in their early fifties. Such early senility, a dementia, became known as Alzheimer's. Later, a doctor referred to this now-common cognitive disorder by that name. It's actually a misnomer, an inaccurate name, but it stuck in the public domain."

Lucille was very worried. She dabbed away a tear. "I'll take him to our home for a while and make other arrangements. My brother won't be happy with that. He feels embarrassed by my father's strange actions and wants all this to be private and personal. He thinks this illness should be kept quiet in our Chinese community. Thank you, Doctor. I'll call that home you suggested."

The doctor shook Lucille's hand and said good bye to her father. "Good for you, Mrs. Chen. I always said that when people get older, they should always make sure they have daughters."

ALZHEIMER'S

A German physician, Alois Alzheimer, studied the brain, especially those with syphilis, which was a very common infection at the turn of the last century.

At an asylum in Frankfurt where he worked, he was asked to evaluate a woman, Auguste Deter, who was just age fifty and suffered from a severe memory disorder, confusion, and disorientation. She died at the age of fifty-one. He concluded that she suffered an early dementia, and on her death, he did an autopsy and examined her brain. After staining the brain to make it more visible under the microscope, he found it was full of black particles, called plaques.

He concluded that the plaques and tangles in the brain were the cause of her dementia. Later, these plaques were found to be a protein called amyloid, and it was thought that this amyloid in the brain was what interfered with neural pathways and the transmission of brain waves.

The conclusion was that this interference produced the dementia, but such an early dementia was, at that time, called presenile dementia. Alzheimer published articles on syphilis, arteriosclerosis, chronic alcoholism, and epilepsy, and focused on the microscopic brain changes causing the clinical manifestations.

A psychiatrist, Kraepelin, later suggested that the specific condition of early presenile dementia be called Alzheimer's disease.

There are two other presenile dementias that occur in the mid-forties with demise by the early fifties. One is Pick's disorder. The frontal and temporal lobes are affected, again due to a buildup of a protein compound. The other is Creutzfeldt-Jakob's, or CJD, caused by a protein called prion. It is believed to be inherited and genetic. It was first described in 1920, and some feel it is similar to mad cow disease.

Thus, what is now referred to as Alzheimer's is a misnomer, since the dementia occurs much later in life. Medically, it is called a chronic neurocognitive disorder.

The ancient "physicians" in Greece and in early Roman times concluded that the early dementias were simply associated with old age. It wasn't until Kraepelin, who referred to this presenile condition in 1910 as a subtype of dementia and called it Alzheimer's.

Unfortunately, for many years thereafter the treatment for this condition was thought to center around amyloid as the cause of this dementia. Thus, time was spent on evaluating the deposition of amyloid in the brain and medication was attempted to be produced to dissolve and remove it.

More recent thinking by some is that this disorder is the result of aging and the loss of adequate blood flow to and inside the brain.

This would occur with cardiovascular inefficiencies, hardening, and spasm of the vessels that could occur in diabetes or other medical conditions, including obesity, that affect the circulation of blood. Prevention and treatment is now focused on this impression.

Also, recent autopsies on the brains of such individuals reveal protein clumps called Lewy bodies and tangled webs of protein causing multiple small, silent strokes. Many authorities are now convinced that this disorder is the result of cardiovascular disease and the lack of proper blood flow to the brain.

Dementia, and specifically this neurocognitive disorder, has now become one of the costliest medical conditions throughout the world. Like other mental health disorders, it is devastating to the individual affected and also to the caregiver, to families, and to the community. Apart from the evaluations and attempted treatments, the cost of nursing home care has escalated immensely.

The greatest cost is the after-care institutionalization. The cost to the family is the burden of losing a loved one, with added psychological and physical fatigue, the cost of home care, and cost of medications. Dementia caregivers suffer from social isolation and severe depression and anxiety, as does the extended family.

Many medications have been developed, but the positive effects are still unsatisfactory. Physical exercise and cognitive mental exercises like crossword puzzles, playing musical instruments, getting involved in educational pursuits and social interactions have been found to be preventative. Diet, avoidance of too much alcohol or use of drugs, weight loss, and maintaining a healthy cardiovascular lifestyle is paramount.

Research has found that the herpes simplex virus may be implicated, and some believe that there may be the potential for vaccines in the future.

There is now the emphasis on early detection with psychological memory testing, but also by analyzing cerebral fluid through spinal taps. However, there is some risk involved.

Early psychological testing in predementia can reveal mild cognitive difficulties such as short-term memory loss, attentiveness, planning, confusion, and abstract thinking. Depression, apathy, and anxiety may be very early signs, together with strange, abnormal behaviors within the family or in the community.

The causes of this disorder are basically yet unknown, but genetics and vascular disorders are possibilities together with the amyloid or protein-development hypotheses.

Dementia, together with diabetes and obesity, are the three major illnesses that are overwhelming our health care system, plus the various medical complications arising from these illnesses and the support required for the care workers and families.

The World Health organization has recently identified several conditions that could encourage the development of dementia. These are physical inactivity, smoking, alcoholism, social isolation, poor dietary habits, diabetes, obesity, high blood pressure, and high cholesterol.

Recent thinking is that there may be a strong link between hearing loss and depression as a precursor, that is, a forerunner, to Alzheimer's. A fear of falling is thought to be an early warning of potential future dementia.

There is strong evidence to suggest that increased social and physical activity, plus group participation and new learning activities, can delay or prevent early dementia. Challenging yourself, taking courses, writing, reading, doing puzzles, traveling, and stimulating your mind with new and interesting activities can be very effective.

Discussing the condition with family members who must be

involved in assisting the caregiver is essential. Research is now centered on the potential use of anti-inflammatories, diet, and weight control.

Finally, a referral to social workers, psychologists, and psychiatrists for evaluation is helpful not only for the affected individual but also for the families impacted.

A full neurological examination is required. Medication is available to calm the affected person in the daytime, and sedatives at nighttime can be helpful. This also assists the caregiver in having a restful sleep without constant interruption throughout the night.

HERPES FOR YOUNG HERBERT

At the walk-in clinic, the doctor spun her swivel chair around in her large, but very sterile, examining room. She was now sitting in front of her patient, Herbert, waiting impatiently and tapping her fingers on the arm of her chair.

"Okay, young man, let's have a look. Drop them," she said impassively. Herbert Rhee had often dropped his pants more than willingly with girls in Seoul before he left Korea to study further, but never to a fifty-year-old woman who looked like his mother.

At least, she looks to be fifty, Herbert thought. Minimum fifty, he was sure, as he looked down at her graying hair tied back in a tight bun. The diploma on her wall had a strange name ending in "ski" that he couldn't pronounce. *Probably Polish*, he thought as he tried to pronounce "Warsikowski" silently to himself.

She reached over to her desk and pulled on translucent latex gloves, and repeated, "Okay, Mr. Rhee; let's see what we have here."

Herby had no choice. His penis was killing him: itchy, painful, inflated like a balloon and red-hot. The nighttime fever and the itch in his crotch were driving him crazy. He'd walked into her clinic that morning—he didn't have an option, as his own doctor was in Miami, at a conference. But a female physician, of all things?

He hadn't counted on that, but decided to comply when his good friend Joo-won said, "Get on with it, before your dong falls off from that raging infection. It will burst like a balloon in your pants. Yuck, swollen and bloated, buddy boy."

Joo-won lit up a cigarette and reared back with the smell. When his roommate looked at Herbie's nakedness after his shower, and added, "Your one ball is swollen like a grapefruit, man oh man."

"I guess I shouldn't have gone with that cute girl at O'Leary's bar two months ago. Seemed nice enough. Reminded me of my young niece living in Seoul. Nice basement apartment."

"Yeah, numb nuts. You saw a lot of her, and yet like your niece, you say? Kinky. Kinky stuff. And no condom, buddy boy. Stupido, stupido," Joo-won said, blowing a puff of smoke away.

Herby dressed slowly. He checked his iPad for the clinic's address again and left his friend telling him how stupid he was.

"Said she was on the pill. Listen, Joo-won, we'll keep all this to ourselves. I don't want our friends or my mother to know anything about this. Right?" He left holding his crotch tenderly and waving the vile smell of Joo-won's cigarette away.

At the doctor's office, Herby pulled off his leather jacket and hung it on the door handle. He prayed that the pretty, young desk nurse who gave him the admission form to fill out wouldn't walk in. She told him to go into the doctor's office and strip down.

He pulled out his shirt, unbuckled his belt, unzipped his trousers, and somewhat reluctantly dropped his pants in front of the doctor who was impatiently waiting for him.

As he stood there in his boxer shorts, he thought maybe, just maybe, he should pull up his pants and walk out. Maybe he should just go home to Korea, where all the doctors were men.

Just then, the doctor grabbed his boxer shorts with both hands and yanked them down to his knees.

"Well, that's it, is it? Aha, you told my receptionist you had a painful hernia. No hernia, young man, no hernia there," she said, lifting up his penis gingerly with her gloved right hand and feeling his testicles with her left fingers.

She shoved a finger into his inner testicular areas with her left hand and told him to cough. When she put her finger deep into each testicle and then up into the inguinal area he winced. But he obediently coughed as he was told to do.

He turned his head away to stare at a large painting of old, historic Warsaw on the wall.

"No. No hernia, inguinal or testicular, but your inguinal lymph nodes are swollen. But, oh, you poor boy, balanoposthitis, Mr. Rhee. And a swollen right testicle. Poor boy, Mr. Rhee."

Herby flinched again as she touched his swollen member and felt his right testicle again. "It's Herbert, Doctor. Herbert. Balano, who? What?" he asked.

"Yes. And you have a fever, I would guess. We'll get a temperature reading. It's from a herpes simplex virus you picked up from some lady. Ah, too bad, too bad, Mr. Rhee. You poor boy, ah … Herbert. Yes, Herbert," she repeated with motherly, parental compassion.

Herbert grimaced again as she lifted his inflamed penis in her right hand and looked at the red-hot foreskin. "Balloon what?" Herbert asked again.

He looked down at his scrotum and hoped he wouldn't get an erection. It was with her warm hands, now holding his private parts, and slowly pulling back on the foreskin.

Herbert was grateful once she let go of his most intimate

belongings. He shuddered with the pain of the retraction.

She rolled her chair back to her desk and took out a prescription pad. She started to write, talk, and pushed a button clipped to the side of her desk all at the same time.

"Rang my nurse to take your temp. It's balanitis, Mr. Rhee. I'll write it out for you with a printout. Infection of the head of your penis, you have there. Posthitis, also; the foreskin, or posthitis, is badly infected. Badly infected by that virus. Testicle infected. That itch in your groin is part of it. Venereal disease."

"VD? You mean VD? Fuck. Oh, sorry. Sorry."

The doctor only shrugged her shoulders and waved it off with her left hand. She continued, "Balanoposthitis means both penis and foreskin. Must be sore. Poor boy. I'll give you a prescription for antibiotics and antiviral creams for the herpes infection."

She was in a hurry. She talked, wrote, found the information on her computer, and whistled a tune as she read it. She pushed the desk button again, threw her gloves into a separate bin, and pushed the print button on her computer. After waiting for the print out, she stood up and handed him a prescription and the computer print-out on balanoposthitis.

"You get burning on urination?" she asked.

"Burning? You mean when I pee?"

She was impatient with that question. "Yes, I mean when you do pee-pee," she said with a smile.

"Yes, burning, burning," Herbert said. He still stood there in front of her, pants down and his inflamed penis now twitching from pain, nervousness, stress, the pressure from her fingers, his stark nakedness, and exposed vulnerability. A cool breeze, wafting in from the open window, added to his body shivering.

He took the print-out and the prescription.

Just as he did this the door opened, and the young, pretty receptionist with blonde hair and freckles walked in. He turned in surprise. She reminded him of the beautiful Adele with the blonde hair, when she took the award for her song in the 007 Bond movie *Skyfall*.

She looked at him, and then her eyes drifted down to his naked pelvis. She didn't register a smile, or even the inkling of a thought about his naked exposure, but only an utterly blank expression. "Put this under your tongue and leave it there," she said dispassionately as she placed the thermometer into his mouth.

He left it there as she waited a minute, took the thermometer out, and read it, showing it to the doctor. The doctor nodded wisely at the nurse, who took another sheet of paper, this one requesting a lab report, from the doctor.

"Okay, Mr. Rhee. Follow me. I'll show you where the lab is, down the hall, for your blood test and penile swab."

As she walked to the door and passed him again, he could smell the alluring perfume radiating from her lithe body, again causing a slight stir down below.

She stopped for a moment, raised her hand a few times, indicating for him to pull up his pants, and beckoned for him to follow. She left the door just slightly ajar.

The doctor scanned Herbert's admission info on her desk. "Ah, yes. Mr. Rhee, it is a fever. It will take some time, but you must follow directions in this print-out. And use a condom from now on in. Are you married? Have a woman you are sleeping with? Or a young man? Having sex?"

Herbert pulled up his shorts, and ever-so-carefully put his throbbing, delicate parts into his underwear. He pulled up his pants, zippered, and then fastened his belt.

As he walked out with his leather jacket on his arm, he answered, "No. Single. No real woman, yet and no ... I ... I did see a young girl for a while. Nice Korean girl," he trailed off, thinking to reassure the doctor that he wasn't with a young man.

"Korean? Good to be with your own kind, Herbert. Listen, you will spread that virus. Human simplex virus. Very virulent, causes cold sores on the lip and possibly throat cancer. Cervical cancer for women."

"Cancer? You mean, real cancer?"

She nodded. "Yes, and tell that 'nice Korean girl' to see a physician for an examination. Now listen carefully to me, young man. No oral, anal, or any other type of sex, and no sex without a condom. Do you hear me?" the matronly physician ordered, wagging her finger at him.

Herbert walked to the door. He opened the door and looked for the young nurse, who was now back at her desk and on the phone.

"Righto," he said, nodding back at the doctor. He said gratefully, "Thanks, doc." He stopped himself from almost adding, "Yes, mother, I heard."

The doctor didn't look up at him. She swung her chair in his direction and handed him a card. "Here: here's the name of a very good plastic surgeon. Call him as soon as the infection subsides. He'll do a circumcision, so this won't recur again. Won't happen again. You hear me?"

Herbert fingered the card as he gripped the door handle with a sweaty palm. It was the idea of surgery, down there, somewhere where it was private. "Yes, I heard. Circumcise me? A surgeon? Will that hurt, doc?" he asked, letting go of the door handle. *Maybe I should just get back to Seoul and my dear old mother*, he thought to himself.

This time she looked up, smiled warmly, shook her head, and replied, "No. Just a little, Mr. Rhee. And only if you get excited with an erection, you know, before it all heals."

Herby knew that the infection, and then the surgery, would only be a small problem in this life experience for him. *My major embarrassment will be keeping this from all my relatives here in the city. Oh, my God ... and from all my good friends at work,* he thought to himself as he left the clinic.

HERPES SIMPLEX VIRUS

Herby had herpes, caused by the human simplex virus and the result of skin-to-skin contact after vaginal sex with his part-time girlfriend who frequented O'Leary's bar. Apart from his symptoms of herpes, he would have also had genital warts, described in an earlier story.

There are two types of the simplex virus. Number one causes the embarrassing facial cold sore, but number two is part of the STD component that causes genital herpes, with all the signs and symptoms that poor Herby demonstrated.

The most common complaints are blistering sores (especially in the pelvic area), pain during urination, itching, fever, swollen lymph nodes, headaches, fatigue, and lack of appetite. The virus can also spread to the eyes after rubbing the affected area and then touching the eyes. Eye pain, discharge, and a gritty feeling in the eyes are common.

As with all STDs, the infected person suffers great anguish and despair with the ongoing infection. This anxiety is passed on to any other intimate relationships that the infected individual has. Long term depression is not uncommon and personal relationships and employment suffers.

Herpes has multiple consequences, some of these serious complications as stated in the story, and these can be very traumatic for the individual. It now has an increasing impact on society, since it lowers the immune system and thus has the potential to cause the person to be more vulnerable to other more serious infections like HIV, especially in certain cultures. This, in turn, produces enormous costs to the medical systems.

Genital herpes can cause serious or even life-threatening infections in the newborn through vaginal delivery if the mother is thus infected. Some STD authorities have also pointed out that this virus makes it easier to contract HIV and other STDs.

Recent studies have found that in astronauts under enormous stress, such stress has reactivated the herpes virus. It is thus considered that those in our population who have extraordinary stress are more prone to the disease.

The number two type of herpes simplex virus is spread through vaginal, anal, or oral sex. The infection may not be symptomatic, that is it is not obvious to the person infected, or to the recipient of that sexual encounter.

Genital herpes can increase the risk of cervical cancer in women. Such cancer can be fatal for many women, but this virus can also be detected in the cervix of many women who don't have cancer. Many physicians therefore suggest that males be circumcised at birth, since the virus or other bacteria can be transmitted during intercourse later in life.

Specialists in STDs reassure women that all women infected with this virus may not be at risk unless they are also infected with the virus causing genital warts: the human papilloma virus. Thus they encourage all women to have a regular Pap smear and laboratory tests.

This chapter will focus in more detail on the human simplex virus and the more serious complications. Such complications are the potential for cervical cancer in women, other genital cancers, and oral cancer.

This sexually transmitted disease has become very prevalent in society because of lack of information, promiscuity, multiple partners, the much earlier age for sexual intercourse, the fact that condoms are not used, and the changes in our culture on sexual behavior, including online dating sites.

Other risk factors in those infected are having another STD that then further weakens the immune system and complicates other medical illnesses that may be present or will develop.

In pregnant women, the virus can spread to the baby during delivery and possibly while the baby is still in the uterus. It does not spread by common items like the toilet seat, as some fear.

The most common types can be prevented with vaccines, but such vaccines should be used in early teenagers. Cervical screening and the Papanicolaou test (Pap) test is essential. These viruses are the most commonly sexually transmitted infections globally.

This, and other similar viruses, have been found in genital and anal cancers. There appears to be a higher incidence of such cancers in homosexual men, and some authorities are recommending regular Pap screening for gay men.

Sexually transmitted forms of this and similar viruses also account for a high incidence of oropharyngeal cancers: that is, of the mouth, upper throat, head, and neck. A regular physical examination of the mouth and throat by the family physician and dental hygienist is highly recommended for both sexes.

Prevention is still the best treatment for these multiple forms of viruses. Vaccines are available, and can prevent the most common types of infection. They are recommended for ages between nine and thirteen, and Pap smears are encouraged for all women to detect cervical cancer. Condoms are essential for sexually active males.

There is no specific treatment for such viral infections. Some infections clear to undetectable levels by themselves with the body's immune system. Nevertheless, the person may still be contagious, and therefore follow-up evaluation is highly recommended.

There are certain medications, both oral and in cream form, that are helpful to reduce the intensity and frequency of the ongoing infection or future outbreaks.

The prognosis or long-term outlook is difficult to predict, since the virus continues to live in the body's nerve cells and may not reappear except with stress. Physical or psychological stress, menstruation, other fevers or illnesses, and sunburn can cause an outbreak after many years of dormancy.

If there is an outbreak, then avoiding any sexual activity is essential. Using the medication as prescribed and washing hands frequently is important.

ANGELINA'S ANXIETY

Angie was fiddling about in her large purse that morning as she and her husband finally found their seats near the back of the Air Canada flight AC608 to Montréal. She brought out her electronic vaper and was anxiously fingering it as she wiped her face of sweat. She grabbed her armrest tightly and watched from her window as the airplane roared down the runway, ready to take off. As a young, dark, Latino woman, she was anxious thinking that the passengers and crew were hostile to Latinos after the problems in the south with Mexicans crossing the border.

"My dear, please put your e-cigarette back in your bag. You can't take it out; the attendant will see you, and we'll be in trouble," her husband, Jake, admonished her. "Here, here's your earphones. Put them on, and it will help you with your anxiety," he added.

"I don't know if I'll make it all the way to Montréal," Angie replied nervously, jamming the headphones on tight and turning on some recorded music.

She put the vape back in her purse, and then gripped Jake's hand firmly. "We should have taken the bus or train from Vancouver like I asked you, Jake," she fretfully said.

Angie had his wrist in a death grip, so he could feel her pulse pounding and see her eyes twitching and her head shaking with her anxiety. "Take another Valium, Angelina. That will calm you down, sweetie."

Angie felt claustrophobic, squeezed tight in the middle seat. Jake was embarrassed, since the elderly, Afro-American man sitting next to the window was fretting with her obvious nervousness.

"I can see that you're a white-knuckle flyer, miss. I have a Tylenol extra strength that I take for my arthritis, if that will help," he asked, offering her the tablet.

Angie looked at him and grabbed the little, white tablet and threw it back with a gulp of water from the small plastic bottle that she was allowed to take on board. Angie whistled and then hailed the stewardess to come over.

"I forgot my Valium in my checked suitcase, Jake. Shit," she said, and then shouted to the attendant who came over. She looked at her name tag. "A double martini, and make it fast, stewardess. Snappy like. Here's my Mastercard, Abigale."

Jake made a motion to Abigale, indicating that his wife was anxious by trembling his both hands in unison. "Sorry, madam. We can't pour doubles. Pay when I bring it," she said kindly, and walked to the back of the plane to prepare her martini.

Angie guffawed and whispered to Jake, "See, I told you. She won't serve us Latinos."

Jake tried to calm her. Her neck was twitching in rhythm to her right eye. The Air Canada plane was now over the Rockies, and the turbulence became quite severe.

"We are experiencing some turbulence, folks. Please remain seated and fasten your seatbelts," the captain said over the intercom as the sign came on to keep buckled up.

With that, a young child behind Jake and Angie started to cry and scream as the plane lurched from side to side. The mother told her child to hush up.

Angie got up and pushed her way across Jake, shouted aloud at the stewardess to hurry up with her drink, threw off her headsets back at Jake, and then ran toward the bathroom. She was crying with fear; mascara ran down both cheeks. "Outta my way," she shouted. "I'm going to puke." She locked herself in. She didn't get to the toilet bowl in time, and heaved her breakfast all over the back wall.

The stewardess couldn't stop Angie in time, since she was also strapped into her seat. She unbuckled herself, got up, and pounded on the bathroom door shouting, "Madam, please return to your seat. The captain assured us that the turbulence will be over soon."

It was a warning that was too late; the smoke alarm in the bathroom went off and wailed for all to hear. Some passengers got up and checked the back for smoke. Children cried.

Angie couldn't wait, and had started inhaling on her e-cigarette as she sat on the toilet seat, wringing her hands and praying to Madonna, Jesus, and the good Lord for safety, or even a parachute.

Two stewardesses unlocked the bathroom door and shut off the screaming banshee on the ceiling. One stewardess called the pilot and told him there was no fire. They both escorted Angie back toward her seat. Jake and the elderly man tried to calm Angie down as Jake held her in his arms, but Angie fought them both off, screaming at Abigale, "We're all going to die. This fucking plane is going down. Let me out of here."

With that she pushed Jake aside, pushed the older man down into his seat as he tried to calm her, threw the stewardess to the floor, and ran to the back. She saw the back door and started to try to push or pull it open. The other stewardess quickly grabbed her and pulled her back to her seat.

The stewardess called out on the loud speaker, "Is there a doctor on the airplane? Please let yourself be known by pushing the button. Thank you."

The older man next to her dabbed her cheeks dry and cleaned the muck around her mouth.

Angie pushed him away. "They're calling the men in white jackets for me," Angie shouted, crying out as passengers around her started to fret.

Jake tried to calm his wife down. She was sweating hard, trembling, shaking, and crying, with spittle flowing out her nose and down her chin. The older man sitting next to her was now just as frightened as she was with the turbulence and her shouting out for Jesus and Mary.

After a few minutes, three doctors came to the back. They all looked at Angie and spoke quietly to the stewardess in charge.

Abigale spoke to the co-pilot, who came to the back at the same time. "Not much help, sir. One doctor is a pathologist, the lady is a radiologist, and the other guy is a gynecologist. We don't have any tranqs on board."

The co-pilot shook his head in despair, turned away from the melee, and spoke to the captain on his radio. "No help from these medicos. We need a damn good nurse or a psychiatrist, Captain Dwaine. None here. We must be near Regina by now, sir."

It was just then that a young girl tapped the co-pilot on the shoulder. "I'm Sabrina, sir. Just graduated as a psychiatric nurse in Kamloops. Can I be of assistance?"

The co-pilot looked at Angie, who was trying to fire up her

electronic cigarette again and then at the stewardess. With a sigh of relief, he took her aside. "The captain said we'll land in Regina. I'll order an ambulance. Here's Sabrina, a damn good, experienced psych nurse who can help. Take the lady with the nurse and get her quieted down in the back, away from the old gentleman before he has a coronary."

Jake had taken the e-cig away from his wife. That action just got Angie more upset, and she ranted and raved about losing her soother.

She just got more anxious, shaking like a leaf, and immediately let go of her full bladder. "My stomach, Jake. It's upset and my heart is leaping out of my chest. My God, I'm too young to die, too young, you hear," she said gripping the old man's arm.

"I heard, missy," was all he said as he lifted his feet away from the yellow puddle seeping toward him on the floor.

The young nurse immediately took charge. She moved Jake away, took Angie by the arm, told the three doctors to go away, and helped Angie up. She escorted her into the back, and told all the gawking passengers to sit down and relax.

"You'll be okay now, miss. What's your name? Come with me and we'll get you cleaned up and get you some water. Poor dear. Must be frightened, are you? Come ... tell me all about it," Sabrina said, pulling her patient into the back area of the plane.

"Angie. It's Angelina. My God, we're going down. I can feel it. Is it a crash landing? Jesus almighty." Angie tried to look out the window, but complied to Sabrina gently sitting her down in the stewardess's seat at the back. She took in large gulps of air as she crossed herself several times and prayed.

Sabrina took Angie's hand and held it. "I'm a psychiatric nurse and you'll be just fine, now. We're not crashing, Angelina.

LAWRENCE E. MATRICK M.D.

We're going to land in Regina, and we'll get a nice therapist for you with some tranquilizers to calm you down. Is your health good apart from your anxiety disorder?"

Angie allowed the stewardess to wipe down her legs of urine and then gave her the towel to clean herself further. Abigale, the other stewardess, gave Angie a small bottle of water and said, "Yes, the pilot is going to land soon, and we'll get you some help, missus."

Angie held Sabrina in a tight grip. "Healthy? Yes, in good health, but always nervous. Heart in my throat, can't breathe, can't sleep, up all night. I wanted to take the train, but my bastard husband refused, lost my Valium … oh, in my suitcase. Yes, nervous since a small kid, I was. I'm from Mexico City. Know where that is?"

Sabrina wiped Angie's brow and patted her on the back. "Yes, I do know. Your parents? Were they anxious people, Angie? Something frightened you as a kid?"

Angie let go of Sabrina and shoved the towel up her pelvis to dry herself further. She looked up at Jake, who had come to the back.

"We're just landing, sweetie. We can visit your cousin in good old Regina and then take the train to Montréal, sweetie. You can see Dr. Parkinson, your shrink, when we get back home," Jake offered. He left when Sabrina motioned to the stewardess to get Jake back to his seat.

Angie watched Jake leave. She pulled Sabrina close to her and whispered in her ear. "My cousin? Piss on him. Wish I could. He's the prick who told me frightening stories of that Frankenstein guy and the Wolfman when I stayed overnight at their place as babysitters, when my parents went to Hawaii for holidays. I couldn't sleep after those stories. Bugger came to my room dressed up as Dracula at nighttime and then fooled around with me as a kid."

Sabrina nodded knowingly. "That got you nervous, Angelina. Did you tell your psychiatrist all about that? That must have made you so nervous as a young girl. Maybe … just maybe you can confront him some day." She added, "Ah, I see we've landed, Angelina."

"No, no. I was too ashamed; never told anyone. I wanted to keep it quiet. You know, hush like. You're the first one," Angie said in a muted tone as the stewardess came to help her and her husband out the back door to the waiting ambulance.

GENERALIZED ANXIETY DISORDERS

G AD, Generalized Anxiety Disorder, is an overwhelming, excessive, and exaggerated anxiety or nervousness, causing worry about everyday life, sometimes without obvious reason. Such uncomfortable complaints severely interfere with the person's total being, both in thoughts and activities. Such an anxiety disorder can be very incapacitating in all aspects of the person's existence.

Anxiety disorders are an umbrella that encompasses panic disorder, social anxiety disorder, obsessive-compulsive disorder, and the various phobias described earlier. Those with GAD often have additional problems with drug and alcohol addictions as an attempt to deal with their anxiety.

The cause is basically unknown yet, but genetics and altered brain chemistry, not yet fully understood, has been suggested.

Thus, a family history plays a significant role. Some medical illnesses may be a factor, like cardiovascular disease, diabetes, neurological or thyroid issues, anorexia, or addictions. Trauma, especially in early life, physical or sexual abuse, family dysfunction, isolation, school or work disruptions, and the overuse of caffeine or drugs can be important factors in causation.

This anxiety, as experienced by Angie, can have traumatic effects on loved ones and extended family. If it becomes overt in social situations, as in the airplane enclosure with Angie, it can produce untoward problems, fear, great confusion, and other traumatic effects for many close by.

Such anxious individuals will take drastic measures to escape or manipulate their environment at the expense of those nearby. This disorder can be very disruptive, not only for the individual but also for their families, and it causes problems in the diagnosis of more serious, underlying physical illnesses for physicians.

GAD affects the way a person thinks, with excessive worry and outright fear of any reasoning powers. There are also many physical issues that are disabling. These include restlessness, irritability, muscular tension, headaches, sweating, nausea, frequent urination, diarrhea, fatigue, sleep disorders, appetite disorder, trembling, breathing disorders, and heart palpitations.

It is a very common malady, and often begins in childhood or adolescence. If there is an early occurrence of the disorder (as in adolescence), rather than later in life, then the condition appears to have a much more significant and chronic effect. If it continues to affect the elder person, then it becomes very disabling as that person has a greater fear of falling, socializing, or otherwise trying to be active.

The disorder will also cause added stress for those afflicted with other medical conditions, like irritable bowel syndrome, neurological conditions, heart disorders, thyroid conditions, pulmonary problems, or musculoskeletal disorders.

It appears to be more common in women, but they are more likely to talk about it openly with others, which can be helpful when compared to men, who try to hide it in overwork, isolation, meaningless activity, or in the use drugs or alcohol.

It may be more difficult to diagnose GAD in certain cultures because the complaints may be totally somatic and variable. That is, the person will only focus on their physical complaints, and they would then be subjected to many overwhelming tests that are inconclusive. There are no lab tests to diagnose GAD, but an evaluation by a therapist or physician can help to make the diagnosis.

Treatment is available with a qualified psychologist or a psychiatrist. Cognitive therapy, that is, the ability to reason concerns and problems out, group therapy, and relaxation techniques are most helpful, and there are a number of medications that can have a calming effect. A consultation and a longer time with that physician may be required to arrive at the best medication to avoid addiction or side effects.

Spiritual guidance with a minister or priest can be very therapeutic. Seek medical help before subjecting yourself to other means often suggested by non-medical professionals.

ANAL ANDY

Yevette watched Andy meticulously pick the small, dark hair off the hem of his white jacket and ever-so-carefully put it into the garbage tin.

"Okay, Andy. I'm leaving. Let's lock up. Time to go soon," Yevette said as she took off her own white jacket and hung it up in the cupboard. She combed her hair and added some lipstick in the kitchen mirror, all the while waving to her husband, Ivan, who was waiting at the door to drive her home.

Andy turned from scrubbing the pizza counter thoroughly. He also waved at Ivan, whom he called "Ivan the Terrible", although he kept that to himself.

Andy saw Ivan to be too gruff: surly, ill mannered, always needing a good haircut, and never having shaved close enough to suit Andy. However, he had no ill-will toward Indigenous people, or to Ivan's position in the local police department as a detective.

However, he liked his boss, Yevette, the owner of the Seaford House pizza café on the outskirts of Prince Rupert in northern British Columbia. She was older than Andy, kindly, like all those

LAWRENCE E. MATRICK M.D.

others he knew from the local reserve when he worked in Prince
George as a chef.

"Just cleaning up, boss. Just cleaning up. Cleaning up the
kitchen," Andy shouted. He then repeated those exact phrases
three times, but quietly to himself.

He liked Yevette as a boss, but not the small ring in her nose
or all the tattoos up and down her arms. *Skinny and no hips, like a
bean pole, and nothing up top*, he thought to himself. She even had
tattoos of fish swimming up one leg, and God knows where else
she had tattoos.

*Maybe only Ivan knows where else. She'll only spread disease from
those dirty, unsightly, bleeding skin sores with the infected tattoos. Yuck*,
he thought to himself, recalling his mother's putrid, stinking skin
rashes on her arms, leftover from needle marks, when she hugged
him as a child.

Yevette knew that the closing ritual would take another twenty
minutes, and that Andy would make sure the door was locked
at least three times. She was well-prepared for that after hiring
Andy a few years ago, when she picked him up hitchhiking on
the Highway of Tears between Prince Rupert and Prince George.

"You're lucky you're not one of us natives, or a woman, off the
reserve on this highway late this evening, fella. Lots of missing
indigenous women who were hitchhiking are never found again,"
she had reminded Andy as he sat there in the passenger's seat,
quietly watching the sun go down.

Andy had taken out his kerchief and wiped the dashboard
down on Yevette's car, and then double-checked the seatbelt for
safety. "Truck broke down back there. I thought I could hoof it to
the city, but thanks for the lift. Many women, you says?"

"You betcha, mister. What's your name, huh? My sister was

one of them. They never did find her."

Andy shifted uncomfortably in his seat. Damn, there it went again. That obsessive tune from the bible his mother used to sing after spanking him for being a naughty boy with the young girl next door. *Jesus loves me, yes I know. Yes, Jesus loves me.*

He tried to stop the rambling thought in his head by double-checking to make sure his seatbelt was on tight. "Andrew. Just Andrew. Cooking. I'm a cook, but got fired. Up in Prince George, I was. Cooking."

Yevette slowed as she approached the outskirts of Prince Rupert. "You're in good shape, big and strong. You work out, does yous? I'll call you Andy, if by rights with you. Give yous a job, too."

She was happy to have Andy, and Andy was happy to work, but she was annoyed that he kept asking her husband, Ivan, too many questions in his work as a detective.

"Never found those who vanished or found them who did the dirty?" he often asked Ivan when he came for pizza and a beer to pick up his wife.

She found his constant questioning irritating, even that day, but she knew that he was obsessed with the violence and wanted details of how the women were killed.

In fact, Andy was going to ask her again, but the idea was interrupted with, *Yes, Jesus loves me, for the bible tells me so.* It went on again and again, over and over in his head. Andy just walked away and cleaned down the cupboards to try and stop the incessant, obsessive humming.

Every day at closing time, Yevette simply waited, organized her menu for the next day, and made notes as to what to order in the morning. Then she got ready to leave with Ivan. She had the last piece of Ivan's pizza and shouted to Andy to close up.

This late evening Andy shouted out, angry and ill-tempered that the pasta bowls were grimy. "Damn old, chipped bowls. Customers will get poisoned. Listen up, how'd he ever get a name like Ivan, being one of your kind, Yevette?"

"Don't throw my bowls away, Andrew. Name? Russian father. He shacked up with a woman on the reserve. Had six brothers and two sisters. Good man, his father. Boris … his moniker—you know, his name. Boris."

Andy watched her leave as that damn tune flooded his brain again. It was all about Jesus in his mind, telling him he should have stayed away from Yevette as a boss and that young girl on the reserve. Maybe he should get out of town. He couldn't afford a baby with that girl now that she's pregnant.

He washed down her counters in the kitchen again and again with the special cleanser that only he had faith in. "Germs Away," it was called, and Andy hated germs, bugs, filth, grime, dust, muck, stains, spots, marks, and grunge of any kind.

Once the counter was spotless, he went over it again, this time scrubbing thoroughly with a wire brush. *So maybe I can stop Jesus from crowing and that girls belly from growing,* he thought, and then laughed to himself.

As he scrubbed, he counted to three hundred by threes, said three Hail Mary's, and then made sure all the labels on all Yevette's cans and bottles in her cupboards were pointing exactly in the same direction, facing him.

"It's done, Yevette. I've turned all the jets off," Andy shouted out to his boss as Yevette left out the back door. But he had to make doubly sure of that. After all, he didn't want the café to blow up in the middle of the night, now did he? That would injure a lot of people.

He not only double-checked the stove, he did it again, a third time. Three was his lucky number. He had learned that in childhood from his mother, who was even more obsessive than Andy was. But she was a good teacher, and being neat and tidy was a perfect attribute in her background culture in Denmark; apart from her smelly dermatitis and her needle marks, of course.

Andy scanned the kitchen one more time. "No bugs or flies, no dirt or grime, let's get those spots, just one more time," he sang as he recalled her mother's little ditty when they cleaned house together as a little boy.

"The water is shut off, the gas oven is clean, the lights will be off, the windows closed tight, the doors locked, and the alarm will be reset." He again went through the litany of jobs: it was a daily ritual, pointing to every item to make certain no one would be hurt, injured, or killed because he was negligent in his duties.

Feeling more at ease after his repetitive rituals, he locked the kitchen doors and went to the men's toilet to wash up. He pushed the jet of soap container exactly three times and then scrubbed his hands. He scrubbed and scrubbed for ten minutes, until his hands were squeaky clean of all bacteria, germs, and viruses, although now raw from scrubbing too hard.

"Now for the nails, ears, hairs in my nose, and brush the teeth," he said to himself, looking in the mirror.

Andy wiped his hands with six paper towels, carefully using only one sheet at a time. The skin on his hands was so dry and cracked from cleaning that he had to use cortisone salves and antibiotic liniments he kept in the cupboard, as prescribed by his physician, after washing. There was only one more act to accomplish.

"Here, Buster. Come now for your brushing. That's a good lad. Good puppy," he shouted and whistled.

Buster came out from under the pizza oven where it was nice and warm and waddled over to Andy.

"You're a good old dog, but old for your years, Yevette told me when she met you."

Buster wagged his tail and stood still while Andy brushed the German Schnauzer until he was good and clean.

"There, buddy. Free of lice, bugs, old hair, and dirt. Just sit while I wash up again," Andy said lovingly to Buster.

He washed again and double-checked the kitchen doors one more time. Light switch off and on three times.

It was only then that he stopped and repeated the Lord's Prayer three times to himself. Just to make sure his mother didn't get in a car accident and his major regrets for taking Buster away from that young girl he picked up on the highway to Prince George several years ago.

"We'll keep all that washing and cleaning to ourselves, eh, Buster? It's all on the QT. Don't want anybody get harmed, infected, poisoned, or injured by our having germs, unlocked doors, fires, dirty pizza bowls, or filth around. Now do we, Buster?" Andy yelled out at Buster and slapped him hard on the rear. The dog yelped and slunk away in fear.

Then it started again, *Jesus loves me yes I know ... for the bible tells me so, yes, Jesus loves me...*

Andy hit himself on the head with his fist to stop that obsessive tune. Buster was dragged along by the heavy chain to the front door. Andy flicked the lights off three times to make sure they were off and then locked the door, checking it again and again.

With the lights flickering, he suddenly felt overwhelmed with thoughts of seeing his mother push the needles into her arms after his father left the family.

He looked up at the sun, still high in the sky that summer day. "Damn. Too bright to go for a ride along the highway today, Buster. Maybe another night."

Buster agreed by wagging his tail and jumping into the back seat.

OCD DISORDERS

Obsessive-compulsive disorder (OCD) is only one of the anxiety disorders that are very common. OCD includes some less common obsessive-compulsive ailments like hair-pulling, skin-picking, jealousy disorders, and hoarding. OCD specifically is considered to be more common in certain cultures and countries where the citizens are taught to be more meticulous, clean, tidy, and well-organized in their overall daily habits.

OCD individuals often learn such habits from their parents and at an early age have certain obsessive thoughts and activities that can trouble them and be overwhelming. It is the repetitive thoughts that are the obsessive component, and the specific, physical routines and activities that are the compulsive element. Together, they form the OCD ailment.

Some obsessive thoughts are fear of contamination, repeated unwanted ideas, aggressive thinking that is uncomfortable, persistent sexual thoughts, images of hurting or fear of injuring others, and ideas that they themselves may be harmed.

As a defense to control the troubling obsessive thinking component, they then develop the compulsive aspect of the disorder. Thus, they have certain compulsions or rituals to try and deal with their obsessive anxiety by constantly checking, counting, repeated cleansing, hand washing, tapping, and arranging, like Andy demonstrated in the fictional story.

OCD, like the other anxiety disorders, can also have a devastating impact on the person's education and employment. Such individuals are unable to complete examinations and get past the first question on the exam, since they focus everything on the earlier questions. Similarly, they have trouble completing tasks in their employment. They impose very strict demands on their families and loved ones because of their OCD.

Many go through such OCD rituals so that they or others don't get harmed by their thoughtlessness or carelessness. For example, Andy was being admonished by his mother for being "a bad boy," and then his anger and hostility toward her was reduced by his obsessive-compulsive rituals. The skin picking, hair pulling, or hoarding activities are active, physical attempts and defensive maneuvers to deal with any uncomfortable, obsessive thoughts. Rituals have a calming effect.

The specific OCD thoughts and activities vary a great deal among individuals, but they all have some common dimensions. An example would be cleaning compulsions to deal with contamination that may harm the person or loved ones. Repetitive thoughts like counting are useful to quell aggression or forbidden thinking like sexual or religious preoccupations.

There is also the body dysmorphic aspect to OCD, where the individual is forever checking their physical features and finding flaws in their facial or other body components. Thus they are forever picking at or asking others (including their physicians) about bodily scars, moles, blemishes, or wrinkles that they have become obsessed about.

The diagnosis is made when there are recurrent thoughts, urges, or images that are experienced and are considered intrusive and unwanted. The person tries to suppress such obsessive thinking by performing some activity that becomes a compulsion. The compulsive aspect becomes repetitive and excessive, but also very time consuming. It is these aspects that make the diagnosis.

The disorder must be differentiated from a specific anxiety disorder, such as those explained in earlier stories, or the result of substance abuse, which then prevents the ability to be in control. A cognitive brain trauma disorder or a more pronounced psychotic disorder must also be eliminated. There may be OCD aspects to all such ailments, but it is the underlying ailment itself that requires treatment.

Some individuals with OCD have a good insight, that is an understanding, that they are impaired, while others consider their disorder as a necessary part of their functioning in life. Some of those individuals with OCD may be able to find employment where their mild disorder is useful and not problematic.

However, a large number of OCD individuals have a lifetime disorder that is disabling. This disorder is more common in males than in females, and with the onset in childhood or early teens.

With OCD there are associated emotional disorders like anxiety, depression, avoidance of interpersonal or social interaction, and drug or alcohol addiction. All such avoidance or addiction becomes problematic in itself, but it is an attempt by the person to reduce or prevent contamination or harm to themselves or to others.

The risk of developing OCD is more common if parents are also predisposed to being overly obsessive. It occurs early in childhood, or later if the individual is more introverted, shy or withdrawn, and subjected to physical or sexual abuse early on in their lives.

The risk of self-harm and suicide is a factor, especially if addictions and isolation follows. Treatment, however, is favorable, but can be prolonged only if the individual is motivated, compliant, and agreeable. Therapy can be found through a qualified psychologist, group therapy, spiritual counseling, or with a psychiatrist. Some receive great benefit from massage therapy, physiotherapy, or acupuncture.

Medication is available through a physician or from a referral to a psychiatrist, who may be more familiar with the proper medication that doesn't cause side effects.

BIPOLAR BIANCA

Cecilia had a key to her sister's condo. She was looking forward to taking her sister out for lunch at the new Vietnamese restaurant around the corner. As she let herself in, she wondered whose fancy car that was parked outside near her sister's house on the street.

Walking in, she turned to find Bianca coming out of her bedroom, dressed in a flimsy, see-through shirt, a flowery hat, and nothing else. She almost ran at Cecilia.

Cecilia threw her arms around her and held her tight. "Hold on, my dear sister. Take it easy. Ready for lunch? Whose car out there?" Cecilia asked, pointing out the window to the silver, topless beauty parked at the curbside.

Bianca whistled and started to dance in time to the music playing from her bedroom. There wasn't much to take off, but she seductively removed the diaphanous garment and pranced in front of the window naked. She waved to some children and their nanny passing by. "It's for you, honey bun. You said you always wanted a topless Porsche, Monte Carlo class. Got it cheap, cheap, cheap like the birds, and the birds love it as they fly over it. You and me will fly to Dallas to see the Cowboys play and then play in the pools. The pool tables are hot in those casinos …"

Cecilia put up her hands to stop her sister. She was very worried about her flighty speech, erratic activity, risky sexual behavior, and spending money like there was no tomorrow. Every finger had an expensive ring on it, her hair was dyed silver with red streaks, her nipples were pierced, she had a ring in her nose, and she was lathered in a strong perfume.

She recalled that her sister had talked foolishly like that eight years ago, when she was high. She stopped her sister in midsentence, which was still rambling and incoherent.

She remembered that her psychiatrist, years ago, called such talk "a flight of ideas." That was when Bianca was admitted and started on lithium for her manic phase.

"Hey, slow down, babe. Take it easy and put some clothes on. I have a car, and don't need a fancy topless like that one. Where'd you get cash like that to buy it?"

Bianca sat down at the table and opened the large drawer. She pulled out a bottle of Jack Daniels and poured herself a tumbler full. "Bank. My inheritance. Cash on the table, two hundred and fifty big ones, and he gave me a discount. There's the keys for you." She laughed hysterically and pointed to a set of keys hanging on a peg near the door.

"My God, woman. You don't have much left in that account. What else did you buy, Bianca?" Cecilia asked, fearing the worst as she took the glass away from her sister.

"Oh, a nice Omega watch, some rings, a few clothes, spa for ten years, and a nice Harley motorbike for yours truly," Bianca replied, taking back the glass and downing half of it in one gulp.

She threw her chapeau off and pitched it in the corner.

"My God, woman. What have you done? You've shaved your head, and are now wearing an outlandish red and silver wig. Our parents in Saigon will be heartbroken. A Harley? Can you take it back? Get your money back?"

"No, too late. Used my five credit cards. Damn banks told me they are all overdrawn. Shit. I sent a photo to our mother. Visiting our grandma in Ho Chi Minh City, she was."

It was just then that the bedroom door opened and a hunk of a young man walked out stark naked. "Can't sleep. What's all the racket about? Who are you, beautiful? Maybe a three way?"

Cecilia blushed and turned away from the nude, statuesque figure and waited to hear Bianca's answer. "She's my sister. Best sister ever, Anthony. Was that your name? Anthony or whatever? No, she don't do three ways, honey." Bianca answered. She smiled and went to him, covering his genitals with her flowery hat.

Anthony, "or whatever," pushed her aside and walked back into the bedroom. He slammed the door hard as Bianca laughed and sang a tune, "Happy days are here again, the skies above are clear again…" as she danced. She agreed to Cecelia's wish and put on some of the clothes that were strewn all over the floor.

"Bianca, who and why is he here? Sorry, dumb question. You'll get pregnant again and have to go back to 'Nam for another quiet abortion. Grandma said that was the last time she'd help you. Who is he? Did he use a condom, for God's sake?"

Bianca started whistling again and called out to Anthony to come for a three-way with her sister.

Cecilia stopped her and moved her away from the windows, wondering if she should call an ambulance.

"Grandma won't see me again because I changed my name

from Bi'ch to Bianca. Means "jade" in 'Nam. My second husband called me "Bitch," and I never liked that moniker that mother gave me at birth," Bianca explained in a sing-song voice.

"Bianca, your present husband, Dac Kien, could be back from his business trip in 'Nam any minute now. If he finds Anthony or whatever here, then you'll be looking for another. Forget about a three-way with that stud. Where are your meds?" Cecilia asked after cautioning her sister.

Bianca wasn't listening. She continued to sing. She opened the drawer again, put on the headsets, and turned up the volume on her iPhone.

She rolled herself a toke from the bag of marijuana she had in the drawer. "Can't hear you, sweetie. Anthony or whatever sold me your new Porsche. Best one I've ever had." She coughed and blew smoke at Anthony as he walked out. He waved at Cecilia, kissed Bianca, and left her apartment.

Cecelia was thinking fast as she took away the headphones. "He's your salesman? Listen, should I call an ambulance and get you to the hospital, or call that psychiatrist, or just drive you there myself, Bianca? You are overspending again, having sex with God knows who, impulsive and erratic and higher than a kite, woman."

"No problem, sister. No worries," she whispered, as though the neighbors were listening.

"Listen, babe. It is a problem now. A major financial one, and maybe more if you get pregnant again. Or get V.D."

Bianca ignored all that, puffed on her marijuana, swilled more Jack Daniels in one gulp, and laughed inappropriately. "No, no. Anthony, or whatever his name was, told me I was a genius. Smart and able to open up a dealership with my money. I gave him a check for five hundred big ones to get started."

"Get dressed. I'll drive you to see Doctor Wan Ho. You liked him. He's our kind from 'Nam, and he'll help you with some meds. I'll stop that check right now," Cecelia said, getting a jacket and other clothes for her sister and then picking up the phone to call their bank manager.

She waited and then admonished her sister. "Listen up, Bianca. We don't want the neighbors or our friends to know all about this little problem you have, now do we? Let's just keep it to ourselves and with the good doctor. Okay?"

Bianca wasn't listening. She tried to dress, but kept dancing hysterically about the room with a phantom partner.

BIPOLAR DISORDERS

Over the past fifty years and more, bipolar disorders were referred to as manic-depressive disorders. The history of that term goes back to the middle of the 19th century, when it was referred to as "*la folie circulaire*" (circular insanity), as presented in a paper in Paris by French physician Jean-Pierre Falret. The German psychiatrist, Kraepelin, studied the disorder in the early 1900s and found it to be composed of episodic stages with intervals of well-being; he called it "manic-depressive psychosis."

It was in the 1960s that the manic phase was distinguished from the depressive phase. It was then that the modern emphasis on bipolarity came into being. The word "bipolar" was later considered to be less stigmatizing than the term "manic-depressive disorder."

There is now simply the bipolar I and bipolar II disorder.

However, these two disorders also include some other categories like cyclothymic disorder, substance abuse/medication-induced disorders, and those due to other related medical conditions.

The major difference between type I and II lies in the severity of the manic episodes. In type I, there will be full manic episodes, possibly without a depressive state. But in type II, the person will experience only a milder form of mania called a hypomanic state, and they will have a depressive component.

A cyclothymic disorder is when a person experiences an ongoing hypomanic period (with depressive periods) that may not be as disabling on and off for at least two years.

The other category, at times with substance abuse and some prescribed medications like amphetamines (speed), some anti-depressants, or some medical conditions like thyroid disorders that are not properly monitored, can produce manic-like episodes of behavior.

During a manic episode, the person suffers a persistent, elevated, expansive mood and increased activity or energy, similar to Bianca's behavior in the above fictionalized story. There is also an inflated sense of self-esteem, grandiosity, decreased sleep, pressure to keep talking with flight of ideas, distractibility, sexual overindulgence, and involvement in buying sprees and foolish, inappropriate business dealings. Social and occupational relationships are severely affected.

Such individuals do not consider themselves to be ill or in need of treatment because they are too indulgent and overly-stimulated. Some may become hostile or threatening, aggressive, seductive, or flamboyant.

In the hypomanic phase, the intensity of the above manic features are less pronounced, but still may be observable by others. It may not affect social or work functioning. In the major depressive component that may fluctuate with the manic state, all the major symptoms of depression are present.

We can see how the bipolar disorder has an effect on loved ones, siblings, and general family as we could with Bianca and her sister. The chaos presented has a traumatic effect on all those involved with the ill individual. Many in the community can be traumatized also, if the person's employment is impacted or if the person is attending an educational system. Mental health systems can be squeezed because the ill person presents with such chaotic behaviors.

In either condition, self-harm may occur and suicide attempts are a very high risk. The disorder often develops in late teens and early adulthood, but may not occur until quite late in life. Throughout adulthood, other factors like substance abuse or other serious medical conditions must be considered.

Some have found that there may be certain increased risk factors, with the disorder being more frequent in high-income earners and in separated, divorced, or widowed individuals. A family history is the most consistent risk factor for this disorder. Females are more likely to experience the depressive components of the disorder to a greater degree than males.

Treatment may be problematic, especially in the manic or hypomanic phase, since the individual feels grandiose and exceptional and therefore may refuse treatment. Hospitalization may be necessary in that situation. However, treatment is available. Some type of medication is necessary, and therefore a family medical doctor or psychiatrist must prescribe the medication.

Lithium was found to be useful many years ago, and was the only treatment available until major tranquilizers were discovered. It is considered that lithium affects the sodium levels in nerve cells and in the brain, and thus lowers the excitation process in manic phases. It is still useful, but other medications that are now added can produce optimum results. Such medications, including lithium, must be monitored frequently by a physician with observation and care as to side effects.

Family therapy is recommended so that members can receive awareness, understanding, knowledge, and support. Individual therapy with a qualified psychologist and group therapy can be most helpful.

IS IT GERRY OR GERALDINE?

"Listen, Gerry, you better take down that name from your bedroom door before Papa gets home. And get that blond dye washed outta your hair, for God's sake. You know how he feels about all this going on now," Roman said to his younger brother as he stormed into the kitchen where Gerry was sitting.

Gerry continued to sit at the kitchen table and didn't look up as he leafed through Nordstrom's catalogue, looking at the clothes of young, teenaged girls. "Yeah, yeah. Maybe, but I like my name. That's my name, Roman. My name from now on in. Hear me? Also, I like this new color," he said, brushing his long, golden locks aside with his hand.

"I heard you, but Papa will flip his lid when he sees those curly girly-girly curls all dyed up like that. The shit will hit the fan, and then you'll be out here with all that crap when the old man gets here. Geraldine? You're nutso man—like many of our Bolshevik relatives were in Russia."

"No need to call me 'man' none no more, bro. They were all brutal men when they killed those pretty, Tsarist girls during the revolution under Lenin and threw their bodies down the well. I'm not like men no more, not brutal like them. I'm Geraldine from here on in. Father can go to Hell. That's why Mamma left him: he's an abuser. I'm not going to be like him, and I may go to live with Mamma when she comes back to Edmonton."

Roman pointed to the teen models in the open catalogue wearing cute dresses, blouses, and wearing high heels. "Listen up, brother. I saw those panties and girly dresses in your bedroom cupboard. You wearing that shit? And high heels yet," he said abruptly and tore the book from under Gerry's hands. He threw it in the nearby kitchen garbage can.

Gerry winced, backed his chair away, and put his hands up to protect himself. "Don't hit me, Roman. I didn't do anything. You hit out just like the old man. Just like a man," he said, crying and moving out of his chair. He picked up the catalogue from the garbage can, brushed it off, and moved to the door, ready to escape from his older brother.

Roman felt sorry for Gerry and apologized. He turned on the oven to warm up the leftover pizza for their father. He had more to say. "I've seen you prancing around your room in those frilly skirts and falling about in those high heels. Trying on a bra. You ain't got any tits."

"I'll have some soon. Nice ones."

"Bah. Bull shit. You should be ashamed of yourself. I don't want my brother seen like that in our neighborhood … an embarrassment to us all. Frilly sissy, girly … like a fruitcake. You better see a shrink."

Gerry backed off further. "Mamma will be back from seeing Grandma in Regina tomorrow. You're gonna tell Papa. Ain't you? Please don't say anything, Roman. The neighbors will hear him beating the shit outta me again for changing. He never wanted a daughter. They'll call the cops again."

Roman set the table for three and turned the oven on high. "You better go live with our mother; she always wanted a girl. Dressed you as a girl when you were youngish. You liked that, didn't you? Disgusting shit."

Gerry thought he could tell his brother something about himself. Something that had always troubled him. "Look bro, the kids at school said I was a 'prissy sissy.' Couldn't throw a football or fight with them. Laughed at me and beat me up when I played with the girls skipping. That was a few years ago. My friends found me sitting in the girl's washroom once last week, Roman. Peeing. Beat me up then, they did."

"Better see the school shrink, boyo. Or whatever you are. Geraldine? Jesus almighty. Father will have a seizure when he sees that on your door. And take off that lipstick. When did all that shit start, with you wearing earrings and frilly rings on your fingers?" Roman asked, pulling at Gerry's ears and grabbing at his painted fingers.

Gerry got up and put his hands up to protect himself. He took out the chicken soup that he had patiently and lovingly prepared for the family. Something mamma taught him before she left. He'd done all of the cooking since then.

He placed the pot on the stovetop and turned it on. "I never liked what I had down below, Roman. You know, all that junk you wear in your pants," he said with a frown and pointed at Roman's crotch.

"You mean what all us good, strong men have down here?" Roman guffawed out loud. Holding his crotch, he pushed his pelvis out at Gerry.

Gerry ignored that. "And I always liked Mamma's Russian

dolls she had in her room. Dress them up all pretty-like. The boys laughed at me when I always sat down to pee in the men's toilet. It disgusted me to pull it out and hold it in my hand."

"Most guys do that, Gerry. Most guys, real men."

"My very close friend, Daniella, will get some of that; what you've got, Roman," Gerry winked at Roman and nodded at his pelvis.

"Daniella will soon be Dan, and we'll be together, Roman. I think that our father knew I spent weekends with Dan," Gerry added.

Roman shook his head in despair. "Our family and the world will never accept lovers like you and Dan, or Daniella, you dumb shit," he spat out angrily.

"Our family and everyone else will as time goes by, brother. Dan and I are marching in the pride parade next month, here in Edmonton. We're going to fight for our rights."

"Geez, kid. That will be embarrassing for us. You better go and see that school shrink. For sure. You always were small and girly-like, and Papa and you will always be in a fight. It's that same old story, over and over: fight, fight, fight. I'm sick of it."

Gerry stirred some chopped up onions into the pot of soup. "Sorry to hear for you, but I did see the school shrinker. She told me, for almost being a sixteen-year-old, I knew what I wanted by now and to see our family doc. Said she wrote our doc a letter when I saw her again for the third time."

"She did? Holy crap, Gerry. Did you? Listen, little brother, our kind will never accept you and your types. Never." Roman shouted, surprised, but now curious about the letter. He helped Gerry finish setting the table.

"Nice guy, Doctor Shamanski. Read the psych report on me that she wrote and agreed to prescribe the meds. Don't tell Papa, or he'll freak out to know I'm on estrogens and have a referral to a plastic surgeon. To build my body up, more female-like and give me some breasts," Gerry almost whispered as he came closer to his brother.

He turned off the oven with the pizza before it burned and slowly stirred the chicken soup as it simmered.

Roman had been to the 'Tranz-Menz' club with his drunken friends years ago and watched the cross-dressers and gays putting on a lavish show as beautiful women. It made him nauseous as his buddies laughed and others hollered and hooted. He'd needed to have a few more drinks afterward to calm down.

"Geez, kid. You mean you're on women's drugs to grow tits? You one of them homo guys, like I seen at that club?" he asked, backing away from Gerry.

"No. Not a homo, Roman. But my body is changing slowly. Got some breast tissue already. Want to feel one?" he asked. He pulled his shirt aside to partially expose his chest. He laughed and enjoyed Roman's embarrassment.

Roman put his hands up and walked to the other side of the kitchen table just in case.

"That good doctor already referred me to a surgeon, like I said. You know, to cut all that junk away."

They heard the front door open as their papa strode in with his heavy work boots on.

Gerry quickly wiped the lipstick off and removed the earrings and pocketed them. He pulled out his baseball cap from his back pocket, pulled up his hair, and put it on his head to cover his long hair.

His father was swearing and cussing and pointing his finger at Gerry. "You cooking again? I told you to order in some pizza. And mow the lawn after school. Why didn't you?"

Gerry moved near to his brother. His favorite tune came rushing into his brain to quell his anxiety. It helped him at times of stress like now, and he hummed as he defended himself. "It was too heavy for me to push around, Papa. Too heavy. I made some of your favorite soup, like Mama used to," Gerry said, getting nervous and moving even closer to his brother.

"You always been a mama's boy. Sissy kid: weak and no muscles. Be a man for a change and go to a gym to bulk up," his father chided as he turned off the stove, picked up the pot of chicken soup, and threw the pot into the sink. "Come on, Roman, I'll take you for some pizza and a beer," he shouted and pulled Roman out the door.

Gerry heard the door slam. He went to the sink and ladled out some soup and chicken bits and put the pot on the stove again. In his head ran that obsessive tune, "As Time Goes By," which he'd heard on the piano in the *Casablanca* movie with Bogart that he'd watched on Netflix months ago.

Humming the tune that calmed him down, he recalled Roman's words about non-acceptance of "his type." *It's just the same old story, a fight of love and glory, a case of do or die. The world will always welcome lovers, as time goes by.*

After his chicken soup dinner, he called his very close friend, Daniella, who was eighteen and already making her legal transition and name change to Dan with a lawyer that Friday.

"Sure thing, Geraldine; come on over, and we can spend the weekend together at my place. My folks are at the lake at our cabin. You can talk to my lawyer on Monday; maybe we can start the process of getting your name and all that legally changed also, sweetie." Dan blew Gerry a kiss and hung up.

The world will always welcome lovers, as time goes by. Gerry chuckled and happily sang the lyrics out loud, hoping that such acceptance in the world would happen—as time goes by. He finished his soup, washed up, and got ready to meet his one and only, Dan.

GENDER DYSPHORIA

There has been a proliferation of newspaper, television, and magazine articles written using various terms related to sexual identity and sex changes. Furthermore, the area has become confusing, since the term "sex" relates to both male and female and, more simply, to sexuality. Thus, the term "gender" is more useful, since some young people are uncertain from an early age as to their "sex" and sexual identity.

The term, gender dysphoria recently became more practical to describe those who have a cognitive (mental) and affective (emotional) discontent with their assigned gender, and thus is included in this book. They experience discomfort because there is a mismatch between their biological sex and their gender identity; this is often called "gender incongruence."

The word "dysphoria" refers to the distress that accompanies the incongruence, that is, the difference, between a person's experienced or expressed gender and their assigned gender at an early age.

Also the dysphoria, that is, the distress, is present if the parents, family, friends, community, or society in general are hostile to the new gender requested, as in the fictional story of Gerry and the abuse he received from father, brother, and friends.

Such family dysfunction is not unusual, since parents and family members find it increasingly difficult to not only comprehend the need, but also try to deal with the potential transformation. This is extremely stressful for the parents and to the rest of the family, especially when they try to grapple with the very difficult and complicated hormonal and future surgical interventions.

Gender dysphoric parents and their children going through the transition stages may be at odds, both emotionally and intellectually with the potential changes, causing enormous family dysfunction, mental anguish and depression. There may also be legal ramifications with court involvement, as parents, depending on the age of their child, may pursue legal opinion if they disagree with their child's request and the physician, psychologist, or psychiatrist's opinions of medications and surgical interventions for their family member.

Parents and others in the family are very anxious about such transformations of sexual identity. It can be very traumatic for the parents especially, but also for siblings and other members to have to adjust. The workplace may have trouble adapting, and if the individual is in school, then ridicule and criticism may be the norm. All of this will add to the individual's stress and anxiety, and could cause severe depression.

It is considered that gender dysphoria has existed throughout the ages, but it is only recently that hormonal therapy and surgical procedures to change one's anatomical sexual organs have become possible. Prior to such possible changes, such individuals were considered to be cross-dressers, strange, transsexual, weird, or outlandish. They had their own cultural and social groups, living in acceptable areas of a large city.

Biological sex is assigned at birth, and is dependent on the appearance of the genitals. Gender identity is the gender that the person "identifies" with or feels themselves to be. Biological sex and gender identity are the same for most people, but not for everyone. Those people whose sex and gender identity are not the same have been referred to as "trans" people or "transsexuals."

Gender dysphoria in children requires a strong desire to be of the other gender, or an insistence that one is already of the other gender. In each case of the boy or girl, there is a need to cross-dress and a strong resistance to wear the typical clothing of that person's assigned gender role. There is a strong preference to play or engage in the opposite sex's toys, games, or activities, and to have playmates of the opposite gender.

Finally, there is a strong dislike of one's sexual anatomy, and a similar strong desire for the sex characteristics that match one's experienced and sought-after gender. Unfortunately, such a person will experience significant distress in family, social, school, and in all other areas of functioning.

Gender dysphoria in adolescence and in adults is similar, except that the adolescent person seeks and expects greater acceptance. They often seek corrective methods for change, either with medication, surgery or both. Such a person at that age may insist on being treated as the other gender, and seek immediate change and acceptance in their new role.

Similarly, they experience significant distress and anxiety in all forms of functioning, either socially, in their occupation, or with friends and family, as was the case with Gerry, who insisted more and more that he was Geraldine.

There appears to be a higher incidence for the need to change in females than in males. As to cultural differences, gender dysphoria has been reported in various cultural societies, but such reporting and open public discussion is problematic in certain societies.

The functional, daily living of such individuals in our society produces problems in all aspects of their existence, and may lead to isolation and rejection of further education or employment. There can be a problem of stigmatization, discrimination, and victimization, with multiple mental disorders and marginalization, especially in resource-poor family backgrounds. Such marginalization may lead to drug addiction, and suicide is a strong possibility.

Treatment in the past focused on having the individual retain and live with their assigned gender and sex. Many therapies were attempted, including massive doses of tranquillizers, hormones, electro-convulsive treatments, LSD therapy, individual cognitive psychotherapy, aversion or conversion therapy, and even prefrontal surgical lobotomy in the distant past. Such gender dysphoric persons were abused, rejected, shunned, and ostracized from family, home, and the community. In some cultures, this may still occur.

Present-day treatment focuses on understanding and supporting the individual, their close relationships (especially their family), and to the wider community. School counselors, family physicians, and all professional therapists are now closely involved in assisting the gender dysphoric male or female. They are all helpful in aiding that person as to potential therapy with changes and to be comfortable with their decisions.

Assessment may be prolonged and may require two or more specialists and several sessions. The family would be involved.

If the individual decides to follow through with hormone

treatments and then surgery, the process is lengthy, hazardous due to possible complications, painful, and possibly problematic due to rejection of surgical changes. The prolonged hormone therapy may produce medical, physical, and psychological complications. Surgical transformation can be costly and unavailable in certain areas of the country.

Transforming the male to female is less complicated, since hormone treatment can produce female characteristics such as breast tissue enhancement, loss of facial hair, and other subtle bodily changes. The male genitals have to be excised with removal of the testicles, scrotum, and penis. The urethra must be maintained for urination, and an attempt made to produce some semblance of a vagina, possibly but usually inadequate for sexual activity.

Female reconstructive surgery to produce male characteristics is much more difficult, arduous, problematic, costly, and very lengthy in scope. Again, male hormones can produce serious complications. A hysterectomy, with removal of ovaries and fallopian tubes, may be expected and the vagina also removed, together with the breasts.

Tissue from elsewhere is required to produce a scrotum, with insertion of some form of acceptable orbs to resemble testicles. A larger piece of muscle, from the thigh, usually, is attempted to be shaped and formed as a penis.

Such attachment is troubling, with a vein from elsewhere required to form a urethra for urination within the formed penis. Rejection by the body of the added piece of muscle is possible, and such extensive surgery can be very painful and problematic.

If all of this occurs and the individual suffers through with the hormonal and surgical process, then a satisfactory, sexual physical relationship can be challenging. However, the long-term prognosis can be optimistic, and there can be great potential for a long, healthy, close and emotional relationship with another loved one for all such individuals.

They will quickly find supportive relationships that are accepting and loving, as Gerry did with Dan. It can be maintained with understanding, support, love, and acceptance as time goes by.

IVAN AND HIS MANY MEDICAL ISSUES

He had just turned fifty, and had another two years on parole. Ivan was looking to make up for lost time after his year in the minimum-security prison, where he'd gotten into a fight and lost most of his hearing.

While at the bar, he complained to his gang buddies about his parole officer's constant nagging about his various medical issues, including diabetes, his skin disorder, arthritis, and his thyroid disorder.

Brutus, his good buddy, was concerned as he listened.

"Listen, Brutus, don't worry. It's all checked out. My blood sugar is A-okay, as I told my parole guy many times. And I take my morphine pills for my arthritis in my hips," Ivan said to his buddy Brutus as he swilled down another beer.

That late morning on the mountain highway, he just wanted to get back on his hog and ride with the boys on this clear, spring day in the Rockies. After drinking three beers at the "Blue Heron" roadside pub and snorting two lines of cocaine in the pub's men's room, Ivan was having trouble with the zipper on his leather pants.

"Need some help with that, big guy?" Brutus, his riding partner, slurred his words outside the pub. He laughed and pointed at Ivan's crotch as he fiddled with the zipper.

Ivan, with his deafness, couldn't hear his buddy, and just waved to the twenty other black, leather-clad gang members revving up their motorcycles. The roar of the men laughing and yelling with motors at full blast shattered the quiet of the mountainside town.

The pub owner was always glad to see them. The gang was happy to buy lots of beer, and he was happy to sell them lots of coke. The locals were just as happy to see them leave after all that noise and rowdy behavior disturbed the quiet, serene village.

Brutus was their leader, and Ivan was proud to ride up front and lead the pack. The rest of "The Blue Angels" quickly formed a line and fell in behind their leaders.

As they came up behind a logging truck making its way to the mill a few miles ahead Brutus waved, cautioning Ivan and the rest to fall back.

Ivan's vision was distorted by alcohol, cocaine, and his fluctuating blood sugar after his many beers. He didn't think he was tailgating the big rig. He waved his buddy off and tried to listen to the music blaring in his helmet.

Just then, the logging truck braked heavily, trying to avoid hitting a boulder that had fallen onto the road. Unable to react in time, Ivan slammed into the back of the truck. He and his Harley slid under the rear axle as the driver continued to brake.

Brutus was faster and more adept, and he swerved around the back corner of the truck and rolled into the ditch.

Ivan was dragged for another twenty feet before the truck driver heard Brutus honking and one of the gang members shouting at the driver in the cab as he came abreast. The truck came to a stop.

Ivan tried to roll out from under the truck, but his legs were useless. He yelled out in pain as his buddies began to pull him and his bike away. They knew they shouldn't move him, but they had to get him out from under the vehicle.

The truck driver called for an ambulance, and finally Ivan was taken to the nearest hospital in Prince George. Brutus stayed with him while he had x-rays and blood work to check his thyroid and blood sugar. He then had an MRI to examine his back and hip pains.

"He has a compression fracture of his lower spine, which gives him the severe back pain and made both his legs numb," the visiting neurosurgeon told Brutus once Ivan was sedated and asleep.

After one month in hospital, Ivan returned home in a wheelchair. Occupational and rehabilitation therapists worked with him at home.

His family doctor prescribed different pain relievers and other sedatives, but Ivan preferred whiskey, beer, marijuana, and cocaine. He even sold his Harley to pay for his drugs. He became severely depressed; his thyroid was underactive, and his blood sugar out of control.

His physician told him he had a chronic pain disorder and referred him to a pain disorder clinic and a drug and alcohol addiction center.

"I'll send you to a specialist for your diabetes and your hypothyroidism. Get your hearing checked," the doctor said, shouting in Ivan's left ear.

Ivan never followed through, since he couldn't hear what was said, and he threw the referral papers away.

Ivan became reclusive. He refused to speak to his pregnant girlfriend or even answer the phone. He kept his blinds closed and wouldn't come to the door.

One day, his buddies and Brutus broke down the door while his girlfriend, Griselda, was at work. They found Ivan in bed:

unshaven, dirty, pants soiled with urine, depressed, and suicidal. They bundled him up and drove him to the pain clinic and got him referred to a psychiatrist.

Brutus was told that Ivan couldn't work ever again after the accident; his legs were paralyzed. Ivan complained that he couldn't even have sex, and Griselda was talking about leaving him.

"Losing my Harley was my last hope for fun in life, Griselda. Maybe having a son and you by my side to wheel me around will help," he pleaded. He swilled down his sixth beer for lunch, and asked Griselda to go out and buy him some more cocaine from Brutus.

Griselda took his half-finished beer bottle and emptied it in the sink. She was already packing her suitcase and was ready to walk out. "I thought you were much stronger; but I don't want my child to see his father as a drunk, addicted and weak in the head. And don't call my mother for help. I'm ashamed of how ill you are and still refusing help. My family is not to know," she shouted as she left and slammed the outside door shut.

Ivan was in despair at living alone. But he continued to fill his prescription for antidepressants, which he found to be sedating and somewhat helpful. Brutus came to visit often with boxes of pizza, hot coffee, and donuts without sugar.

He spoke to Ivan as he took the pizza out of the cardboard box. "Look Ivan, see the situation from a more positive perspective—that you survived when you could have very easily been killed in that accident; that you are going to be a father, and you may see your child occasionally. And that, by going to the pain disorder clinic and seeing a psychiatrist, you are taking steps to improve your health, buddy." Brutus never mentioned a drug addiction therapy center.

Ivan wasn't sure what Brutus was saying. "I guess. My thyroid is normal now and diabetes stable."

Those words from Brutus were not that meaningful for Ivan, since he was in such pain, was deaf, depressed, his memory was poor and his blood sugar was not, in fact, stable. His major sorrow was the loss of his bike, his girlfriend, and the drugs that Brutus no longer brought him.

MEDICAL ISSUES CAUSING MENTAL DISORDERS

A number of physical medical issues that precipitate mental illnesses have already been outlined in the preceding stories and chapters. Those addicted to illicit drugs and alcohol eventually suffer from severe depression, anxiety, phobic and panic disorders, and potential early dementia. The various medical disorders producing sexual impotence and marital dysfunction that accompany such addictions are not uncommon.

Recent observations on traumatic brain injuries in football and soccer players have found that such players suffer from chronic traumatic encephalitis (CTE), a neurodegenerative disease caused by repeated head injuries. Mental disorder symptoms include multiple behavioral problems, mood disorders like chronic depression, and serious problems in thinking.

Cardiovascular conditions have the propensity to precipitate anxiety and panic if there is a shortness of breath, irregularity of the heartbeat, or chest pain. Depression appears to be a natural physiological component following a cardiac emergency such as a heart attack or following heart surgery.

Similarly, any respiratory condition like asthma, bronchitis, chronic obstructive pulmonary disorder, or pneumonia that cause a shortness of breath will induce anxiety due to the fear of apnea—that is, shortness of breath. Panic naturally overcomes the person in such disorders, and such panic can become chronic, requiring psychological therapy.

Those afflicted with diabetes can also suffer severe fear, anxiety, obsession over diet and panic if their blood sugar levels are fluctuating and not maintained. As blood sugar levels vary, fatigue, severe anxiety, or depression can follow.

If thyroid levels are not maintained, then the low thyroid condition called hypothyroidism causes similar psychological symptomatology. A high thyroid level, or hyperthyroidism, can cause overstimulation, tremors, and anxiety, possibly requiring other medical or surgical treatments.

Orthopedic, bone and spinal disorders, severe arthritis causing ongoing pain, and a sleep disorder as Ivan suffered in the fictionalized story above cause depression and have the potential for medication or drug and alcohol addictions. Ongoing chronic pain disorder is very fatiguing and depressing, as the person is sedated with medication and fears going out to socialize or being active lest they fall and injure themselves further.

Very similar mental disorders develop following muscular disorders like amyotrophic lateral stenosis (ALS), and multiple sclerosis (MS) due to the person's lack of mobility and socialization, again requiring medication for the long-standing depression.

Parkinson's disorder now has a better prognosis with medication, support groups, and physical therapies. Any such psychological disorders mentioned, such as anxiety or depression, respond quickly to therapies that are now available.

Ongoing genitourinary disorders with bladder weakness for men and women become very depressing. Women suffering from chronic menstrual dysfunction are often overwhelmed with chronic depression, which then requires psychological therapy and medication.

Cancer in any part of the body, including the brain, in either sex or age can require lengthy, frequent evaluations, chemotherapy, and surgery. Such ongoing therapeutic measures have their own complications, but the severe anxiety of waiting for results can be devastating in itself for the affected person, as well as for loved ones and family.

Having to deal with such ongoing physical medical issues is a major test of anyone's stamina and willingness to cope. They must continue to seek treatment, be hopeful, and persevere. Now, compared to many years ago, there is hope and help in so many areas of our society, with professionals who are available to assist and support the mentally ill and their families. Close, intensive, interpersonal therapy is available through family physicians, counselors, psychologists, and psychiatrists.

Support groups, hospital outpatient clinics, physiotherapists, massage therapists, chiropractors, and pharmacologists are now trained to assist and support such medical illnesses that cause mental grief. Spiritual guidance is readily available through your religious affiliation. Medications are more therapeutic than ever before, and with fewer side effects.

"When we honestly ask ourselves which person in our lives means the most to us, we often find that it is those who, instead of giving advice, solutions, or cures, have chosen rather to share our pain and touch our wounds with a warm and tender hand. The friend who can be silent with us in a moment of despair or confusion, who can stay with us in an hour of grief and bereavement, who can tolerate not knowing, not curing, not healing and face with us the reality of our powerlessness, that is a friend who cares."

- Henri Jozef Machiel Nouwen

ABOUT THE AUTHOR

Dr. Lawerence E. Matrick received his degree in Medicine from the Manitoba Medical College, and then worked at the Provincial Mental Hospital as a resident in psychiatry. He continued his studies in London, England and received his British degrees in Psychiatry, and later his Fellowship in the Royal College of Physicians, Canada. As an Assistant Professor in Psychiatry at U.B.C., he also had a full-time private practice in Vancouver for almost 50 years. Qualified by the courts, he often attended as an expert witness, dealing with those involved in motor vehicle accidents.